The NAME SHE GAVE ME

Betty Culley

HARPER TEEN

An Imprint of HarperCollinsPublishers

HarperTeen is an imprint of HarperCollins Publishers.

The Name She Gave Me
Copyright © 2022 by Betty Culley
All rights reserved. Printed in Lithuania. No part of this book may be used
or reproduced in any manner whatsoever without written permission except
in the case of brief quotations embodied in critical articles and reviews.
For information address HarperCollins Children's Books, a division of
HarperCollins Publishers, 195 Broadway, New York, NY 10007.
www.epicreads.com

Library of Congress Control Number: 2021950887
ISBN 978-0-06-315783-5

Typography by Julia Feingold
22 23 24 25 26   SB   10 9 8 7 6 5 4 3 2 1
❖

First Edition

To anyone searching for their true home—
wherever that may be

You got to walk that lonesome valley

Well, you got to walk it for yourself

Ain't nobody else can walk it for you

You got to walk that valley for yourself

—Traditional gospel folk song

PART

One

Rynn

NAMES

My birthmother was twenty
when I was born,
four years older
than I am now,
and she gave me a name.

Scheherazade
(Shuh-hair-ah-zod)
has three *e*'s,
two *a*'s
and twelve letters.

Mom and Dad changed my name to
Rynn—
four letters, one repeat,
and no vowels,
unless you count the (sometimes) *y*.

I don't love the name
Scheherazade,
but my birthmother
gave it to me.

It's the only thing
from her
I (don't) have.

SCHEHERAZADE

My lost name is a clue,
like a message in a bottle
washed up on an empty shore.

In an old book,
a girl named Scheherazade
told a king stories
so he wouldn't kill her.

Night after night,
she stopped her stories
in the middle,
like a soap opera
or a detective series,
and continued them
the next night.

It took 1,001 nights
and 1,000 stories
for the king to fall in love
with her.

Why she would want to marry
a man who killed women
is beyond me.

Or why she'd want
to be with someone

who took 1,001 nights
to figure out he loved her.

I'm wondering if my birthmother
wanted me to know
that in order to survive
without the truth
of who I am
and where I came from,
I would also have to make up stories
to get me through the night.

HOLES

I don't know if I got
my gray eyes,
or my straight brown hair,
from my birthmother.
I don't even know
her name.
At eighteen,
I can get my original birth certificate,
genetic and medical information.

Until then,
I can only guess
why she gave me up
and why I was born
with so many holes.

A hole in my throat,
A hole in my back,
A hole in my heart.

The hole in my throat,
a cleft palate,
took two surgeries to fix.
Before they closed it
I had to drink thickened milk
or I would choke.

The hole in my back—

a sacral dimple—
is not cute
the way you'd think
when you hear the word
dimple.

It's a tiny tunnel
on my spine
that ends in darkness.
It goes nowhere
and doesn't bother
anybody.

They only found
the hole in my heart—
an atrial septal defect—
when I was thirteen
and started being
out of breath.

That makes me wonder
what else is wrong with me,
what other defect
they haven't found yet—
another missing piece,
or a part that stopped growing
before it was done.

Defect and *perfect* are so close,
only two letters apart.
If you say them fast,

defect perfect defect perfect,
they almost sound the same.

I can't help it—
I want everything back.
I want my lost name.
I want all my vowels.
I'll even take the hole
that they closed
in my throat—
round and perfect
as a little ring.

I wish I still had
my heart *defect*, too,
so I could tell people
how I feel
all the time,

There's a hole in my heart.

8

SECRET

For nine months
I was inside my birthmother—
then I wasn't.

My baby brain
might remember her voice
or her heartbeat,
but I don't.

Then I was in a foster home
for six weeks
before I got adopted.
I don't remember that, either.

I never told anyone,
but when I was in elementary school
I always looked around
for my birthmother.
I thought she could be
anywhere.
If a bus driver I didn't know
waved at me,
or a woman clapped really loud
at the end of my school play,
I guessed it might be her.

For a while I thought
the school secretary

was my birthmother,
because she acted extra nice.
I thought maybe she'd gotten the job
just to be near me.

Sometimes I pretended
my birthmother
was like God—
she knew all about me,
but was waiting
for the right moment
to appear.
I was pretty sure she'd come
on my tenth birthday—
double digits and all.
Or when I had my first period.
Or when my heart got fixed.

Even though I knew
my adoption was *closed*—
that no one could tell her
where I was—
it took a long time
for the truth
to sink in.

This year I definitely knew better,
but the day I turned sixteen
I was still disappointed
there was no mystery present
stuffed in the mailbox.

That's when I knew
it would have to be *me*
searching for *her*.
That maybe all these years
she'd been waiting
just like me—
to be found.

I did think how I'd feel
if she had a great new life
and didn't want
to hear from me,
but I figured it would hurt
just as much
to learn that now
as later.

So I started asking
why my adoption was closed,
like a locked door
with no key
to open it,
and why I had to wait
two more years
until I'm eighteen
to find out about
my birthmother.

Mom did not like hearing
the word *birthmother*,
but there was no other way

to ask.
Finally, a secret shot out
one sentence
after the other,
like a fire catching hold,
as Mom finally told
what they kept from me
for nine years.

This birthmother
you keep asking about
kept a baby she gave birth to
seven years after you were born.
A half sister
from a different father.
The agency called us
during the pregnancy
to see if we wanted her.
We said yes,
we'd take your sister,
but then your birthmother
changed her mind.

Now the fire
burns in me
that I spent all those years
not knowing about my sister,
the one who was
good enough
to keep.

SISTER

She'd be nine now.
Maybe she's called
Jacqueline or Antoinette
or Evangeline—
all names
with five vowels too.

I don't hold it against her,
being the one who got to stay.

If we met,
would it be like
looking in a mirror?

My face, her face.
People might say to us,
I can tell you're sisters.

Although I can't show her
the hole in my heart,
I'd let her listen
to the whoosh of blood
going past the place
they patched it up.

MOM

Mom and Dad tried to have
their own bio baby,
but it didn't work out.

I've seen the ultrasound prints
Mom has hidden—
of the babies
that stopped growing
before they were born.

Maybe those babies
would have made her happy,
but I can never
get it right.

It's been this way
as long as I can remember—
but it's gotten worse lately.

There's no way to predict
what will make Mom angry,
what will calm her down.

I can get in trouble
for leaving the room
or for staying,
for saying sorry
or not saying sorry.

If I speak too loud
or too soft.

If I move
too slow or too fast.

In other words—
no way to win
no way to stop
what's coming.

They say babies don't come
with a manual—
but neither do parents.

CURSED

When I was little
I once heard Mom tell Dad,
I'm cursed.

He put his arms around her.
Not true, Leanne,
he answered,
You're a blessing.
A blessing to me.

But I believed her.
I was young enough
that Dad still read to me
before bed,
and I'd heard the stories—
a girl turned to solid gold,
a boy with a swan wing
for an arm,
shoes that kept dancing,

So I thought a witch
or a wicked queen
or even a jealous friend
had cast a spell
on Mom—
like the one where splinters of glass
from a magic mirror
got into a boy's eyes and heart

and made him think
the world was ugly.

Only Mom's curse was
something like:
You shall not find happiness.

In the stories
there was always a way
to undo a curse.

It could be as simple
as a kiss
or a flood of tears,
or as hard a task
as climbing a mountain
of glass.

So I thought up ways
to break Mom's curse.
Once I washed her car
with a bucket of water
and a big sponge.
I even cleaned the dirt
off the mud flaps,
and the grime from
the tire rims.
When I was done,
I was so excited
to show her
how it shined.

She was happy
with her clean car—
but the happy didn't last.

GARLIC FARM

My birthmother asked
for me to grow up
on a farm.

There weren't many farmers
in central Maine
looking for babies,
but my father
had started growing garlic
the year before.

It turned out
garlic was good enough
for the adoption agency.

Before they brought me home,
Dad put a sign
at the end of our driveway.
"GARLIC FARM."
The *A* in GARLIC
and FARM
were drawn to look
(take a guess)
like bulbs
of garlic.

That fall
he planted a half acre

of garlic.
Garlic is backward this way—
you plant it in the fall
and it comes up the next summer,
surviving all winter
under the snow.

It turns out Dad was smart
about garlic.
People pay a lot for it.
But I still think
a garlic farm
is a fake farm.

So this summer
I'm working as a babysitter
on a real farm
down the road.

My birthmother
wanted me on a farm,
and I want to see
why.

This farm is more than
a half acre.
It has fields in all directions—
huge fields full of corn
and other real crops.

It has tractors and balers,

and its own gas tanks
to fill them.
It has greenhouses
with plastic walls,
and a whole building
just for pigs.
There's another building
next to it
full of chickens.
I'm only babysitting
the farmers' boy,
but I'm still on a farm.

The boy is almost two
and his name is Douglas—
a good mix of
vowels and consonants.
His hair is dark brown,
like his eyes.

When I first met him,
he'd just woken from a nap,
but he put his chunky arms out
for me to hold him,
and I got the job.

When I told Mom and Dad about it,
Dad said,
That sounds like fun.
Isabel and Big Doug are good people
and innovative farmers.

Mom shook her head
and made a face.
If you want to spend your summer
changing diapers and chasing chickens,
that's your choice.

I knew the problem wasn't chickens
or even babysitting.
It was that I made a decision
for myself
without asking her.

THREADS

I don't have an exact date
for when I started to lose hope
that I could make Mom happy,
but it might have been
when I was twelve,
the time I made the placemats.

When I was growing up
Dad taught me to sew,
and for her birthday that year
I made placemats for Mom
on the treadle sewing machine,
starting the wheel
with one hand
and treadling with my feet.
It took me days
to finish them all.

On the morning
of her birthday
I picked daffodils
from the garden
for the breakfast-in-bed tray
Dad carried in to Mom,
and handed her
the wrapped box.

I actually held my breath
while she opened the present,

waiting to see
how she liked it.

Mom didn't say anything
about the fabric or the stitching,
or the outline of garlic
I'd sewn into each corner.
Instead, her fingers found
the few stray threads
I'd forgotten to cut.

Get me a scissors, Rynn,
she said,
holding out a thread,
and I'll fix these.

I'll do it,
I said,
taking the box back
and hugging it
to my chest
as I left the room.

I put the placemats
under my bed,
and Mom never asked
where they were.

I could have trimmed the threads
myself
and put them on the table—
but I didn't.

Eventually, I threw them out
in the bottom of the trash
Dad took to the dump,
so now they're probably somewhere
at the bottom
of the Beacon landfill.

RULES

My first day babysitting
I ask his mom, Isabel,
what the rules are
for taking care of Douglas.

She blinks,
and I think she's trying
not to laugh.

Isabel is also *from away* like Dad,
but even farther than New York.
Douglas's dad, Big Doug, grew up here
on the farm,
but Isabel is from the Dominican Republic,
she told me,
where it was warm enough
for a mango tree to grow
in her backyard.
Here she can grow apple, plum,
and even peach trees,
but not mango.

Isabel speaks Spanish to Douglas,
and he speaks it back to her.
I took Spanish I in middle school,
but I still can't speak it as well
as a two-year-old.

Rules?
Try not to let him
bite you,
'cause it hurts.
Take him for walks,
he likes that a lot.
And he loves to play ball.

Now it's me
trying not to laugh,
because she just described
how to babysit
a dog.

Yeah, that's about it,
Isabel says, and adds,
and just keep him safe.
She's taller than me
and her black hair
hangs down to her shoulders.
She waves her arm
in a circle
at the big farm around us,
as if it's full of things
out to get
a little boy.

DOUGLAS

Before nap time
Douglas likes to wrap
the ends of my hair
around his fingers
and stick them in his mouth.

It's like a pacifier
the way it soothes him.
My long hair
puts him
right to sleep.

And sometimes when I carry him,
he puts his hand
down the front
of my shirt.

That boy,
Isabel laughs
the first time she sees him do it,
he loves his boobs.

I must have looked surprised,
because she goes on to explain,

He does it to me,
but I never saw him do it
to anyone else.
It's a comfort thing.

Okay, I say.
If the space
on my skinny chest
where cleavage would be—
if I had it—
gives him comfort,
it's fine with me.

And I turn away
so she can't see what's happening
to my face—
because although I remember
Dad holding my hand
on walks in the woods,
and carrying me up high
on his shoulders—
I don't remember this feeling
from when I was little—
my mother's body
being a comfort.

GARLIC BAGS

The real farm
has a wooden farm stand
along the road,
and a sign that says:

CSA FARM SHARES PICKUP
FARM STAND OPEN
TUES/THURS 1–3 PM

There's a metal hanging scale
to weigh the tomatoes,
peppers, string beans,
cucumbers, and potatoes.
Isabel also sells jars of dill pickles
and dilly beans she cans herself.

Dad doesn't sell his garlic,
garlic vinegar, and garlic scapes
at a farm stand.
He sells them at fairs
and farmers markets.

His signs for the market say,
"Heirloom Garlic" and
"Artisanal Vinegar."
Once I heard a woman
ask her friend
what "heirloom" garlic meant.

The friend said "heirloom"
was a fancy word for
expensive.

Dad puts the garlic
in little cloth bags
he sews himself
and he draws a garlic bulb
in permanent ink
on every bag.

If you look close,
every drawing is different—
like each time
he saw something
he never noticed before
in the same bulb.

Dad knows people in town
call him "Garlic Man"
behind his back,
but he doesn't mind.

I do grow garlic,
even if they think
it's not a real crop,
he explains to me.
No need to take offense.
In fact, maybe I'll make myself a hat
that says "Garlic Man."

NO, I shout,
picturing exactly the kind of hat
Dad would make—
a straw hat with felt letters
and a piece of garlic
tied to the brim.
Please don't.

DAD

He was already so old
when I was born—
almost sixty—
people think he's my
grandfather.
He actually walks
a little bent over
like an old person,
and his hair is white.
I was his last chance
to be a father.

It's been so long
since he was a child,
he's mostly forgotten
what it was like.

Or being a child
was different back then.

We didn't have that.
We didn't do that.
We didn't know that.

To hear Dad talk,
he was born in the
dark ages of childhood,
when people were still

figuring out
how to be children.

You grew up in the Bronx.
What cool city things
did you do?
I asked him once.

It took him a minute
to think that far back.

We slid down the cobblestones
next to the city steps
on pieces of cardboard,
and my brothers set fire
to scrap wood in an empty lot
next to our apartment building.

Cobblestones. Scrap wood. Fires.
See what I mean?

It's not just *Garlic Man*
Dad doesn't get.
It's like he missed
the part of growing up
where you learn
how teasing works.

Once I told him the name
a kid at school
said his father
called Dad.

Flatlandah

Dad looked at me with his
pale-blue watery eyes.
(I used to think he was born
with dark-blue eyes,
but they were fading to white
like his hair.)

Flatlandah?
That's the name
they called me?
he said.

Yes, is it bad?
I asked.

It could be worse,
Dad answered.

Later on,
there were other names—
names I stopped telling him about:
House-husband
Gentleman farmer
City slicker
Jew

Mom was born in Beacon
and lived here for three years,
until her mother left.
But even though Saul Parkman

has lived in the same house
for twenty years
and cuts all his own firewood
by hand,
he's still
from away.

Mom might think *ungrateful*,
but Dad would understand
why I need to get more information
about who I am.

Because there's one thing
we have in common—
we both ended up places
where no matter
what we do,
we'll never truly
belong.

LITTLE PILGRIMS

My adoption agency is called
Maine Home for Little Pilgrims.
It was originally an orphanage
and a place for girls to hide
when they were pregnant.

There's an online form
on their website
for making an appointment.
If I can get in the door
where the files are,
I will be as close to the truth
as I've ever been.

I've had sixteen years
of being told I was chosen,
instead of the obvious fact
that I was given away,
and I'm ready for *open* now.

Even if what's in the files
is worse
than I can imagine.
it will be my worse
and no one else's.

When I tell them
I'm not pregnant,

not going to deliver
a new little pilgrim
for them to give away,
they might be disappointed.

But then I'll say *I'm*
one of their little pilgrims
come back to the Home
after all these years.

JUNE

My best friend, June
(two vowels, two consonants,
no repeats, and a month),
says she'll go in with me
to the Little Pilgrims appointment,
but I want to go alone—
the way I was the last time
I was there.

June Tibbetts
is the anti-adopted.
Everywhere she looks,
literally,
there's someone related to her—
sisters, brother, aunties,
uncles, cousins, grammies,
grampies, nieces, and nephews.

Where are MY grammies?
I once asked Mom.

Dead and gone,
she said.
Your father's mother, Rivka,
who you're named for,
died before you were born.
And your other grandmother
is gone somewhere
only God knows.

June Tibbetts lives on Tibbetts Road
in Beacon,
if that's a clue.
Hundreds of acres
of woods and fields
with enough room
for generations of Tibbettses
and their families.

She lives with her mother,
who was born a True,
and her brother, Terence
(triple *e*'s like me).

A year older than June,
Terence got his GED last year,
and works with his father
selling firewood.
He knows I don't love school
the way June does,
and he likes to joke
that there's always a spot for me
in the firewood business.

June's parents divorced,
and her dad moved into a trailer
across the road.
Back in the woods
is her sister May's house.
Over the hill,
her oldest sister, April,

and her children.
Somewhere in all that land,
there's a place waiting for June
if she wants it someday.

It's not all that great,
June says,
when I tell her how lucky she is
to be surrounded by relatives,
people who look like her.

Yeah, she says,
I can see what's gonna happen
to my face
in twenty years,
or my memory
in forty.
And how I won
my mama's high forehead
and total inability to draw
in the genetic lottery.
Oh, and my crooked bottom teeth.
Thank you so much for that,
Grammie True.

June exaggerates.
No one pays attention
to her forehead
'cause they're looking into
her beautiful green eyes
that don't judge.

And the only thing they notice
about her smile
is how happy it makes them feel.

She may not excel
in art,
but she can do math in her head
I can't do on paper,
and she can explain
why you see light from stars
that burned out long ago.

Before June started school,
Mrs. Tibbetts had a home daycare
called Wee Ones.
I stayed with June and Terence
and the other "wee ones"
when Dad was busy
and Mom was working
at the post office in Chester,
so we got in the habit
of playing at her house,
even though I had
my own big room
at Garlic Farm.

I never said I liked it that way
because then it was easier to pretend
I was a Tibbetts, too.

MOM, MEET MOM

When I first told June and Terence
about my Little Pilgrims appointment,
June asked,
What will you do
if you find
your birthmother?
Will you introduce her
to your parents?

I'd like to see THAT,
Terence said.
He spun his tall body
back and forth,
gesturing with his hand.

Mom, meet Mom.
Dad, meet other Mom.

I realized I hadn't thought
that far ahead—
to my birthmother and Mom
in the same room.

Who would I stand next to?
Who would I introduce first?
Would my birthmother tell everyone
about being pregnant with me?
Would Dad tell the story

about bringing me home
for the first time?

And would we all meet at Garlic Farm,
or where my birthmother lives,
wherever that is,
or at some neutral place
like Switzerland?

ALEXANDER

Douglas and I are playing
in his plastic swimming pool
on the front lawn
when Isabel's car
pulls into the driveway.

The swimming pool
is only a foot deep,
but for Douglas
it's like the ocean.
I'm in my old red bathing suit,
so faded it's almost pink.

He makes waves,
I make waves,
and we pour water
over each other's heads.

That's what we're doing
when a boy
pulls a rolling suitcase.
out of the back seat.

It's hot out,
but he's wearing a long-sleeved
blue button-down shirt
and tan dress pants
with sharp creases.

His short brown hair
and brown eyes
are an older version
of Douglas's.

Rynn, meet my son Alex,
Isabel puts a hand on his arm.

I wave from the pool.

Not Alex, Alexander.
Not son, stepson,
he says.

Even though Mom
would call that rude,
I like him right away.
He defends his long name
(nine letters, three vowels, two *e*'s)
and is a stickler for the truth
(stepson, not son).

Isabel's face is more sad than mad
but her hand stays on his arm.

Alexander, this is Rynn.
She's helping with Douglas
for the summer.

Rynn R-I-N or Rynn R-Y-N
or Rynn short for

something else?
he asks me.

Douglas pours a plastic bucket
of water over my head,
and it takes me a minute
to catch my breath.

It's Rynn R-Y-N-N,
but my original name,
the one my birthmother gave me,
was Scheherazade.

I don't know what made me say that
to Alexander.

His chocolaty eyes
study me.

Hi, Scheherazade,
he pronounces the four syllables slowly,
I'm here for the next two weeks.
Hi, Douglas,
he waves to Douglas,
who's so excited
he throws a bucket of water
in the air.
I can call you Scheherazade,
if you want.
It helps to call things
by their right names.

I don't know if that's a dig
at Isabel
for calling him son
instead of stepson,
or just random advice
from the universe
coming to me from this
serious brown-haired boy.

Son, stepson
Open adoption, closed adoption
Sealed, unsealed
Chosen, given away
Holes, perfection.

Alexander is right.
It matters
what you call something,
even in your mind,
because it becomes
what you name it.

Yes, you can do that,
I answer.
You can call me
Scheherazade.

POSTER BOY

On the way to the adoption agency
I sit between Terence and June
in the front of Terence's old pickup.

He glances over at me,
his green eyes as kind as his sister's.
Terence grew to six foot three
in middle school,
and even though he didn't pick fights
or bully anyone,
the boys knew not to tease me,
because he had my back
as much as June's.

After they drop me off,
Terence and June will wait for me next door,
in Goodwill—
another place people bring things
they don't want anymore.

There's a wooden suggestion box
and a basket of blank cards
on the wall where you first come in
the Maine Home for Little Pilgrims.
My suggestion would be:

"Find a better name
for this place.

Maybe one that shows you know
we live in the twenty-first century."

It might be my imagination,
but the woman at the desk
looks at my flat stomach
a little too long.

And you are here for . . . ?
she asks.

I have an appointment.
I emailed Ms. Boothby.
She said one o'clock.

The big clock on the wall
reads five minutes to one.

And your name is . . . ?

Rynn Parkman
Scheherazade

Which one?

Both,
I say.

Have a seat, then,
I'll let her know,
she nods,
as if I've come

to the right place
to have two names.

I'm the only one
in the waiting room.
There are posters
on all the walls—
full of babies, toddlers,
older children, teenagers,
and grown-ups.

My favorite is a boy
around ten years old
standing next to a man.
They're holding hands,
but they're not looking
at each other.
They're not looking away,
either.
The boy doesn't look happy
or unhappy.
His expression says,

Things are happening to me.
I don't know why or how.
There's not much
I can do about it,
but that's okay.

When I leave
I could write on a card
for the suggestion box—

that they have more posters
like that one.

I want to cut out the boy
from the rest of the poster,
and hang it up
in my bedroom.

I try to figure out
how it's attached
to the wall,
if I can lift up the edges,
but I don't see any tacks
or tape to pull.
I take a picture of the boy
with my phone
and edit it,
so you don't see the writing
on top of the poster:

"CREATING FAMILIES"

I gently touch his cheek.
He tells me,

I was dropped
here on earth.
The people around me
say things, do things.
There's no way
to get back to my planet.

My face is very close
to Poster Boy's
(I want to answer him,
but I don't know
what to say)
when my names are called.

Rynn Parkman. Scheherazade.

EMILY, LCSW

The woman who calls my name
is standing there
watching me touch
Poster Boy's face.
I'm Emily Boothby.

She's wearing jeans
and a black blazer
and holds a tan folder.

I'm wearing a red sundress
and white flip-flops.
There are little red hearts
on my flip-flops
that you can only see
when I take them off.
My hair is in two braids.

She leads me into her office.
I can tell it's hers because
there's a sign on the desk:
"EMILY, LCSW."

Emily Lick-Swah?
I read out loud.
The name LCSW
could have been
on my parents' short list
for me.

Lick-Swah?
she repeats,
making a puzzled face,
and I point to her sign.

Oh, LCSW stands for
licensed clinical social worker.

She doesn't go
behind her desk.
There are two armchairs
facing each other,
and she sits in one of them.

Have a seat,
she says,
and I sit in the other chair.
Emily Lick-Swah
balances the folder
on her lap.

We're so close
I could reach out
and touch it.

How can I help you, Rynn?
she asks.

I want to know more—
about my birthmother
and the sister she kept.

Emily Lick-Swah
does a pretend peek
in the folder,
too fast to really read anything.

You're sixteen,
she says.

I don't know
if she's asking me
or telling me.

Yes, that's true,
I agree.

Unfortunately, you probably know
by Maine law I can't tell you anything
until you're eighteen.
Unless we have signed consent
from both your adoptive parents.
I'm sorry.

I don't know if it's hearing
what I already know,
or the quiet way she says sorry,
but suddenly I'm crying so hard
it feels like I'm choking
on my tears.

With the hand that's not
holding the folder,

Emily LCSW takes a bunch
of tissues from a box
on the little table between us
and passes them to me.

But, I cry, *but,*
and I pull at the front
of my dress,
they fixed the hole in my heart,
but—it feels like
it's still there.

Her face changes,
and I realize she's looking
at my scar.

Three years ago
when they found
the hole in my heart,
I had a surgery,
and now there's a white line
straight down my chest
that looks like the chalk pen
Dad uses on dark fabric.

Only, water doesn't make my line
disappear.
Alexander must have seen
the line
when he saw me in the pool.
It's not always the first thing

people notice about me—
but usually the second.

I don't hide my line.
My sundress has a V-neck,
and the line
goes right to the bottom
of the V
and beyond.

Emily Lick-Swah looks sad
to see the place
that surgeons
cut my chest,
like she's thinking
about all the things
that can happen
to a little pilgrim
once they leave the Home.

SURRENDER

It takes me a long time
to stop crying.
The cries come from a place
so deep inside me,
I didn't even know
they were there.
So it takes a while
for them to go back
where they came from.

Of course, if there's a new medical issue,
she says,
*your parents can request
medical history information.*

Is that my Little Pilgrim file?
I point to the folder
she's still holding.

What?

Everything I say
seems to confuse her.

*I'm one of your little pilgrims.
Don't we all have a file?*

This?

She holds up the folder.
This is just what the secretary
at the front desk
printed out for me.
Your name and date of
surrender.

Surrender?
One word
and the tears come rushing back
like the tide,
with no way to stop them.

I stand up.
I feel how wet and red
my face must look
to her.

She's my own sister.
My own mother,
I say before I run
from the room.

I don't look at the secretary
at the front desk,
but I slow down
when I see Poster Boy
watching me.

Surrender,
his eyes say,

is just a word,
even though he knows
neither one of us
believes that.

BELLY BUTTON

June and Terence
are sitting in the truck
outside Goodwill.

June studies my face.
No luck?

No, I shake my head,
they're really good
at not telling you anything.
Unless I can get both my parents'
permission.

June ties her loose red hair
in a ponytail,
and takes my hand
in hers.
Terence reaches across June
to tap my shoulder,
then starts the truck.

I'm babysitting today,
so we head back.
Terence turns the radio on,
then turns it back off
so it's quiet in the truck
all the way to Beacon.
Four exits on the interstate,

then the familiar turns
past woods and fields
that take us to the farm.

Douglas screeches
when he sees me.
It's a happy screech,
like he thought
he'd never see me again—
yet here I am!

To be honest,
Douglas also screeches at a cup
full of juice,
his green toy dump truck,
and his own belly button.

Every time he finds the circle
in his belly,
just big enough to fit his finger in,
he's thrilled.
I made the mistake of showing him
he's not the only one on earth
with a belly button,
so now he screeches
when he sees mine, too,
and fits his little finger
in the place
that used to connect me
to my birthmother.

Right now,
I'm glad I'm wearing a dress
and not my two-piece bathing suit.

I don't want to be reminded
that the connection is gone
and all that's left
is another blind hole
to mark where it was.

WATER SLIDE

I'm not in the gifted and talented program
like June,
and I didn't join the team at school
that made Lego robots
and went to the state competition,
but I invent a new game for Douglas
I call Water Slide.

I set his plastic slide
so the ladder part
is on the outside of his plastic pool,
and the slide part is on the inside.

I get in the pool
in my sundress
and cheer Douglas on.

Climb, Douglas!
Slide, Douglas!

Every single time
he lands his butt
in the water
with a splash,
it makes us both laugh.

Isabel comes out of the greenhouse
to see what the excitement is all about.

Mira, Mami!
Douglas calls to her,
and does Water Slide Number 42.

This is brilliant, Rynn,
you're really a natural
with kids.

I don't say that technically,
I'm still a kid,
or that water plus slide
is not genius,
but I'm happy for the
compliment.

A-gin! A-gin!

Douglas climbs out of the pool
and back up the ladder
of his new water world.

The screen door slams
and Alexander stands there
on the front porch
watching us.

It's fine if your friends visit
when you're here,
Isabel leans down
and whispers to me.

It's always a difficult time
for Alexander—
being on the farm.

Isabel doesn't say
what the *difficult* is,
and I don't ask.

But I realize what I recognized
in Alexander's eyes—
a worry he thinks he's hiding
from the world.

Alexander comes down
the porch steps
to Water World.

Scheherazade
in a kiddie pool
in a red dress,
he says
in his fact-stating way.

I look up at him and
answer,

Alexander
on the farm
eleven more days.

SCIENCE AND MATH

There aren't any hot spots
or magma chambers
in Maine,
and the town of Beacon
isn't over a fault line
or along the Ring of Fire,
but when you live
with a mom
who can explode
without warning,
you're always waiting
for the next eruption.

Until eighth grade earth science
I didn't have the words
to describe what it was like.

Then Ms. Harris showed us slides
of volcanoes.
One was the Mayon volcano
in the Philippines.
There were wisps of smoke
coming from the top,
but the grass below the volcano
was bright green
and wildflowers grew.
You could see thatched-roof houses
and people tending their crops.

Why would anyone live that close
to a volcano,
someone in class
called out,
unless they had a death wish?

Good question,
Ms. Harris said.
Can you think why
that might be?

I didn't raise my hand,
but I could have answered.
I would have said,
People stay there
because the soil is fertile,
the black sand beaches
are beautiful,
and it's the only home
they've ever known.
And because they hope
the last eruption was really
the last.
Or they think,
if it does erupt,
they'll be fast enough
to outrun the ash.

Then I'd say
that even though the bottoms of your feet
become extra sensitive to heat and rumbling,

like a human seismic monitoring device,
don't let your guard down.
There are times
even your feet
will fail you.

Ms. Harris told us one in ten people
in the world
live in the danger range
of volcanoes.

There are 3,154 people
here in Beacon.
Even I can do
the math.

SECOND CHANCES

One time, when I was young enough
to still ride in a cart in the supermarket,
a man said to me,
You should be as pretty
as your mother
when you grow up.

I didn't know if he was making
a prediction
a wish
or a demand.

That still happens—
people trying to find bits
of Mom's beauty
in me.

Mom sits at the kitchen table
on her day off.
She's wearing a white dress
and her hair is twisted in a knot
at the back of her neck.

The parent permission papers
for the Home for Little Pilgrims
are folded in my back pocket.
I figure it's as good a time
to ask as any.

I turn the gas on
under the kettle.
Would you like some tea?

People used to make offerings
to the gods
to keep volcanoes from erupting.
They lit incense and put rice and fruit
in little boats
and sent them down a river—
maybe they still do.
But Mom loves tea more than
rice and fruit.

Sure,
she answers,
and I choose her favorite teacup,
pour in the hot water from the kettle,
dip the tea bag up and down
to release the flavor,
add the milk.
Then I set it carefully on a coaster
in front of her,
take the papers out of my pocket,
and hold them up.

Dad already signed,
I say,
but I need you to sign the forms, too,
so I can get information
about my birthmother and sister

from the Little Pilgrims Home.

Mom doesn't reach for the papers
to see what they say.
Instead, she points a finger
at my chest.

*We didn't fix that heart of yours
just to break it again.*

I cover my heart
with my hand.

*I don't care
if it breaks,*
I answer.
I need to know.

Well, I care, she says,
*so you'll have to wait.
I'm not ready
to open our family
to that woman.
You may not understand it now,
but some people
don't deserve
a second chance.*

I feel a sharp pinch—
like the point
of a sewing needle—

in my heart.

Wouldn't YOU want a
second chance?
I answer,
I know I would.

And as I head outside
I hear the shatter of Mom's teacup
on the tile floor.

SCAPES

Dad is out in the garlic.
With his bent-over back,
old plaid work shirt,
and thin flyaway hair,
he looks like a scarecrow
someone dressed up
and stuck in the middle
of the garden.

Each long row has a different
kind of garlic.

I run my hands along their stalks—
Glenora Pearl, Siberian, Persian Star.

Elephant garlic has the biggest bulbs.
Orchard Hill has purple stripes.
Extra Hardy keeps all winter.

Dad is cutting the scapes—
the twisty green tops
that end in a miniature garlic
of their own—
to sell at the farmers market.

I know the theory—
by cutting the tops off,
more energy goes to the bulb

still growing under the dirt.

But I never like seeing
the prettiest part of the plant,
curving and reaching for the sun,
cut right off.

I walk down Siberian,
up past Glenora Pearl,
and stop in front of Dad.

I told her you signed,
but Mom won't do it.
Why didn't you ask the adoption agency
more about my birthmother?
All I know is my name
and that she wanted me
on a farm.

Dad rubs his hand
back and forth
across his forehead,
as if he's trying to activate
old memory cells
in his brain.

Mom didn't want to know.
She said she didn't
see the need.
You were going to be ours,
after all.

But I remember your birthmother
was studying to be a vet tech.

Dad holds the basket
full of curly garlic scapes
under one arm.

Do you have to be so ruthless?
I ask him.

What do you mean?
He squints into the bright sun
behind me.

The scapes,
I point to the basket,
do you have to cut
every last one?

HEAT WAVE

The day after my visit
to the Home for Little Pilgrims,
Douglas and I are asleep
on the couch in his living room,
when there's a knock
at the door.

It's ninety-four degrees
on the outside thermometer
and there's no AC
in the farmhouse.
Everyone is calling it
a heat wave.

Douglas lies on top of me,
and one side of his sweaty face
is stuck
to one side of mine.
His fist holds a piece of my hair
to his mouth.

They're asleep,
I hear Alexander say.

I can see that,
June answers,
and I open my eyes,
as Alexander lets June
in the house.

You know what, Rynn,
June starts right in,
forget the Little Pilgrims,
and what's in some stupid file.
When Grammie True got into genealogy,
she found all these dead relatives
looking through old books
in the public library.
Think what you could find online.
You could do your own research.
Find your whole family.

In June's world,
everyone's business
is everyone else's business.
She's used to all the Tibbetts and Trues
having a say
in her life.
As friend of a Tibbetts,
I get the same deal.

If you need help,
I'm extremely good with
computers,
Alexander offers.

As am I.
Very good with technology,
June answers,
like it's a contest.

I doubt either one of them suspects

how many times
since my birthday
my fingers froze
over the keyboard—
wanting to find out
but too afraid to try.
Scared what it would feel like
to find nothing at all.

You're right, June,
I say.
And think how proud Grammie True
would be if I found something.

June laughs and makes room for herself
on the end of the couch
next to me.
I put my feet in her lap.

Alexander moves the standing fan closer to us
and turns it on high.

Douglas sighs in his sleep
and pulls my hair
into his mouth.
I softly pat
his bug-bitten back,
and despite the heat,
I start to feel the burning places
inside me
cooling down.

SPRINKLER WORLD

When Douglas wakes up,
June shows him what she brought.
It's an old sprinkler
connected to a coil of hose.

Vuss dat?
Douglas asks her.

Douglas, my boy,
June tilts her head at him,
why do you talk like a baby vampire?

She sets the sprinkler to oscillate
back and forth, back and forth.
I'm almost jealous
how much Douglas loves
Sprinkler World.

And Douglas learns some new words
from June.

Dammit, Douglas, you're the man,
June says
when he daringly runs through
the middle of the sprinkler spray.
His own *Dammit*
echoes loud and clear.

Isabel told me Garlic Farm

is your place,
Alexander says to me.
I've seen the sign,
but I didn't know you lived there
or that your family grew
garlic.

I do. I live there
and my dad grows the garlic.

Rynn's father is very inscrutable
and very precise,
June says.

She's adjusted the sprinkler spray
so now it's only about
a foot high.
Douglas leans over
and tries to drink from it.

My brother, Terence, thinks
Rynn's dad was a spy,
June tells Alexander.
Rynn, remember when your dad
talked about fishing
in the Aleutian Islands
and visiting tea plantations in Ceylon.
And doesn't he speak
all those languages?
He used to work
for the government, right?

I think so,
I say,
a long time ago,
before he moved to Maine.

I know exactly what June means
by *precise.*
The careful way
Dad measures the distance
between garden rows,
using sticks and string
to lay out the furrows.
The way he pins his fabric
so evenly.
It's like he doesn't know how
to do things messy,
even if he wanted to.

And inscrutable—
how you can't tell
what he's really thinking
or how much
he notices.

Inscrutable and precise,
Alexander repeats.
For me, my two words
would be bionic *and* analytical.

June walks over to Alexander
and looks him up and down.

Alexander,
is this your way of telling us
you're really a robot?

Alexander peers back at her.

Hmm, that question makes me think
analytical *might be one of*
your words, too, am I right?

I don't know,
June says,
turning away from him,
and it seems like
something about the question
bothers her.
When I figure out
my two words,
I'll let you know.

What about you, Scheherazade,
Alexander asks me,
what are your words?

Scheherazade?
June gives Alexander,
then me,
a look.

Her birthname,
Alexander explains,

ignoring or not noticing
June's surprise.

I face my best friend.
Yes, my birthmother
named me
Scheherazade,
I say.

Oh, she nods,
as if it makes perfect sense
that my name was Scheherazade.
And if she's hurt
to find it out
from Alexander,
it doesn't show.

All these years,
I never spoke about
my lost name.
The shame of losing it.
The shame of wanting it.
But now every time I say
Scheherazade,
a strange thing happens—
a piece of my name
comes back to me.

So, what are your words?
Alexander repeats.

June and Alexander
are both looking at me now.
Alexander with his *analytic* face
and June with her familiar
Tibbetts/True face.

Mine? Mine?
I stall for time.
I guess they'd be
Babysitter and Garlic-Girl.
And yes, I know Garlic-Girl sounds like
two words, but it's hyphenated.

June and Alexander laugh
at the words I come up with
instead of *damaged* and *abandoned*.

Me plash,
Douglas announces his trick.
He does a belly flop
into his plastic pool
and comes up smiling.

My words
for Douglas
are *joyful* and *trusting*.
Two things
it's hard to be
on Volcano Island.

FARMERS MARKET FAMILY

May to October,
Saturdays are farmers market day
in downtown Beacon.

Dad calls the group of people
set up in the parking lot
behind the laundromat
our farmers market family.

Carlton selling maple syrup
and maple sugar candy
out of the back of his truck,
Francine setting out cheese samples,
Vincent and Hugh
stoking the outdoor pizza oven.

We get there early,
put up the white shade tent,
lay out the baskets of garlic,
arrange the bottles
of garlic vinegar,
hang the signs,
stack the garlic bags,
and open the quarter rolls
into the money box.

My favorite farmer is Francine.
Her hair is as white as Dad's

and she wears it in a bun
on top of her head.
She trades her cheese for Dad's garlic
and also sells pumpkins
in the fall.

Francine knows a magic trick
to make name pumpkins.
With a sharp nail,
scratch letters on a pumpkin
when it's little.
The letters grow
with the skin,
and when it's finally harvested,
you have a personalized pumpkin
with an engraved name.

Dad says Francine has a daughter
who hasn't been home
in twenty-five years,
but she still makes her
a name pumpkin
with "Zoe" on it
every year.

I go over to her booth and
hand her a piece of paper.

Francine has samples on a tray,
with a sign that says "lemon cheese."
I taste the sharpness of the lemon

and the sweetness of the cheese
all in one bite.

She reads what I've written.

She-he-rasad? Ski-hera-sade?
Is this a name?

Yes, Scheherazade,
I pronounce it slowly.
Can you write it
on a pumpkin?
I'll pay for it.

There's been a pumpkin for me
with "Rynn" on it every October
as long as I can remember.
But there's no rule I know of
that says only one
name pumpkin
per person.

Francine folds the paper carefully,
and puts it in her front overall pocket,

Will do,
she says,
and no, you can't pay me.

PRINTS AND CIRCLES

What do you know
about your adoption?
Like, where you were born?
Or your parents' names?

Alexander and I
are at the kitchen table
on the farm.
Douglas is upstairs
taking a nap.
The baby monitor is on
so I can hear
when he wakes.

Not much.
I was born in Maine
and my birthmother was twenty
when I was born.

I don't tell him
about my sister.
I'm trying to find
the truth,
but still keep
some pieces of it
for myself.

What about your birthfather?
he asks.

I know even less about him.
Supposedly, he was "not involved,"
I air quote the words.
So if he didn't want a baby,
he's definitely not going to want
a teenager.

I don't actually know
what "not involved" really means.
Not interested?
Not ready to be a father?
Not aware I exist?
Not a nice guy?
And there's this,
I touch my line.
I had a hole in my heart
that they patched
a few years ago,
and I also had
a hole in my throat
that got fixed
when I was a year old.

Alexander very politely
looks at my line
like it's the first time
he's noticed it.

What does it feel like?
he asks.

No one ever asks

about my line.
Mostly they pretend
they don't see it.

It feels like skin.
You can touch it,
if you want,
I say.

I lean across the table
far enough for him to reach,
and he gently touches
the top of my line
with the tip
of one finger.

It feels really delicate,
he says.

It's not, I say,
it's just skin
that grew back together
to make a line.

He takes his finger off.

There should be a better word
than line,
he says.

You're all about the words,

huh, Alexander?

I make my hands into fists
to stretch the skin on top
and hold them out to him.

See, I have lines on my hands, too.
If you look really close,
you can see them.
They're like the footprints
bird feet make
in the snow.
They're from all the IVs I had
when I was a baby.

He brings his face level with my hands
and studies them.
He traces the tiny white lines.

Prints,
he says,
that might be a better word.
Scheherazade
with bird-feet prints
in the snow of her hands.
So you're all good now?

I think so,
I answer,
but I don't say
that maybe they haven't found

what else is wrong.

I have lines, too.
Or maybe not lines.
Circles,
Alexander says.

He holds out his right hand.
I turn it down
then up again.
Like the prints
on my hands,
his are hard to see.
Thin circles
where you'd wear a ring—
the width of my line,
the color of my prints
around his pointer
and middle fingers.

Alexander looks down at his hand.
I was five.
I heard them talking
in the Life Flight helicopter
to Boston.
My fingers were
in a cooler.
"Yeah, another Maine
table saw accident
heading your way.
No, this time the guy

is smart enough
to keep his own hands
where they belong—
but dumb enough
to let his kid get hurt."

After the accident
they got divorced.
And ever since,
when I visit here,
I'm not allowed to work
on the farm.
That's their deal.

Alexander looks down
at the fingers on his right hand—
at the rings that aren't rings.

What about mowing the lawn?

Are you kidding?
Combustion engine. Sharp blades.
Heck, I went to make a smoothie
in the blender
and Isabel watched me like a hawk.

And you go along
with the deal?
I ask.
Aren't you old enough
to decide for yourself

if you want to cut
more fingers off?

I'm serious
when I say it,
but the way it comes out,
I can't help laughing.
I cover my mouth
and try to apologize,
but I'm laughing too hard
for words to come out.

Alexander smiles.

No one ever put it
quite like that.
But then I'd be breaking a promise
to my mother.

Can I ask you something?
he says in a quiet voice.

Sure,
I answer.

He holds out his hand again.

Can you look at my fingers
and tell me if these two
seem any different
from the others?

Be honest.

Alexander points to the fingers
with the circles.

I touch each finger
one at a time.
I almost think
he is holding his breath,
waiting for my answer.

They all feel the same,
different lengths,
of course, one's a thumb,
but no real difference.

He holds up
the two circled fingers.

They were in a cooler,
he whispers,
like he's five years old
again.
A cooler.
They were gone
from me.
Parts of me,
gone from me.

I've had so many things
done to me

in hospitals,
I know exactly
how to answer.

I take his right hand,
and press it flat
against the length
of my line.

I feel the heat
of his hand on my skin.
and I look him right in the face.

There's nothing bionic
about you.
No matter what they do
to your body,
you are still you.
Still your hand.
Still your fingers.

Then the baby monitor crackles
and I rush upstairs to get Douglas
before he wakes
to find himself alone.

LEGACY.COM

When I was little,
Dad sewed new curtains
for my attic bedroom
and dyed them sky blue.
My windows face the back
of the house,
and look out on
rows of garlic.

I open my iPad,
and even though I'm alone,
it feels like June is here with me,
cheering me on,
wanting what I want.

I try all kinds of searches
with combinations of
adoption, Beacon, Little Pilgrims, Maine,
Rynn Parkman, Leanne Parkman, Saul Parkman.
Even *Emily LCSW* and *Garlic Farm.*
I type in *cleft palate*
and *Central Hospital.*
I try *Scheherazade* and my birth date.
Then when I tap
Scheherazade and *Beacon, Maine,*
I get one hit
with both *Scheherazade* and *Maine.*

It opens to a page
with a flickering candle
and the words "Legacy.com"
above them.

Under the candle,
there's a photo of a woman
that takes my breath away.
Below it are these words:

*PORTLAND, MAINE—Scheherazade "Sherry"
Worthen, 33, passed away unexpectedly on Monday,
September 21, 2015. She was born on July 11, 1982, the
only daughter of the late Yvette and Curt Worthen.*

*She attended Portland public schools and graduated
from Portland High School.*

*She loved camping and the ocean. Sherry is survived
by her daughter, Ella, her brother, Curt Worthen Jr.,
and her precious dog, Storm.*

*A graveside service will be held at Riverview
Cemetery, River Road, Portland, Maine, on Saturday,
September 26.*

*Arrangements under the care and direction of Obert
Funeral Home.*

*In lieu of flowers, donations can be made to the
Humane Society of Maine.*

The photo is black-and-white,
like the photos
of the other dead people
on Legacy.com.

I touch the screen
with my shaking hand.
Even though I'm in color
and she's black-and-white,
our eyes
are the same shape
and her mouth,
in a half smile,
looks just like mine
when I don't want
my picture taken.

I read it again,
ignoring all the dates
but one,
and count it
on my fingers.

She died the year I turned twelve.
So she would have been twenty
when I was born,
just like my parents said.

Four whole years
she was gone
and I didn't know.

Her own daughter
never got to go to her funeral
and cry for her.

Although the daughter she kept
and her precious dog, Storm,
are mentioned,
I'm nowhere to be found
in the obituary.

I have a sister,
and now I know her name—
Ella (two vowels,
four letters, and one repeat).

Scheherazade "Sherry" Worthen
gave me the best clue
I never guessed.
She gave me her name.

Sorella

Facts

My caseworker, Roshni,
tells me Dad was in a fight
in jail, and the other person
got hurt bad.

Who STARTED the fight?
I ask,
and Roshni says
she doesn't know.

She says Dad has to stay in jail
even longer,
and it would be good
to find me a family
to be with
until I grow up.

I tell her
I want to stay
right here.
Martha knows about
foster kids.
The rules are easy.
Be kind.
Pick up after yourself.
Use your words.

I can call her Martha,
not Mom.
She's big around the middle.
And she calls my mother
my "mama."

Every year
on the day Mom died
Martha says a prayer,
and all the kids
are quiet
for a while.

*Do you want to talk
about your dad, Ella?*
Roshni asks me.
No, thanks, I say.

People can make you do
a lot of things,
but they can't make you talk.
If they try,
it's called torture
and that's a fact.

Bling

Martha put a picture
of Mom
in her prettiest photo frame.
There's crystals all over it,
purple and red and white.
They look like real jewels,
but Martha calls it
bling.

I know where Martha hides
birthday presents,
and I think I know
which is the one
for my tenth birthday.
It's a locket that opens
with space on each side
for photos,
and there's bits of
green bling,
my favorite color,
on the front.

Big

Martha's doctor
put her on sugar pills
'cause she's too big.
I wanted to taste them
but she said they don't taste sweet
at all.

The other day Martha said
she knows why
retired has the word *tired*
in it.
I said I would play by myself
and let her sleep
anytime she wanted.
For some reason,
that made her cry.

I'm her last foster child,
she said.
Last and best,
I said,
and that's a fact.

Martha's husband was named Blaine,
and he died from his appendix
before I came.
An appendix is the size of an earthworm
in your belly,

and no one needs it anyway,
Martha says.

Blaine's photo is over the TV
in the living room
so he can be part of
pizza-night Fridays
and popover Sundays.

I don't want
to get to know
a new family,
with new rules
and new food.
I want to stay
with Martha
until I'm eighteen,
and that's the only fact
that matters.

Gabe

The first night he came to Martha's
Gabe cried really hard.
And the second night, too.
He wanted to go back
with his mom.

I thought maybe his mom
was in jail, like my dad.
So I asked what his mom
did wrong.
And he screamed *Nothing*
at me.

So I told Martha
I tried to make friends
with Gabe,
but he only cried
and screamed.

Remember when you first came?
Martha said.
You cried, too.

Yes, I said,
because it was different here
and I didn't know if I'd like it.

How do you think Gabe feels?
she said.

So I wrote a list for Gabe
of all the fun things
he could do—
Pet Poker Face
Take Gravy for a walk
Help Martha cook
Jump on the trampoline
Pizza-night Fridays

Gabe wanted to do
everything on the list
all in one day.
So even though it wasn't Friday,
Martha said Gabe could help
make pizza.

And I don't know
which thing worked,
but he didn't cry that night.

Mimi

My foster sister, Mimi,
came to live at Martha's
last year.
Sometimes she acts bossy
like she's MY big sister,
which she's not.
Then I say her name
should be spelled
ME-ME.

She's gonna be
the next to last kid
to leave
when she goes to college
in September.

When you leave,
I get your bedroom,
I tell her.

Mimi is gonna study
to be an engineer.

Like a train engineer?
Choo choo!
Gabe teased her
when she told us.

What kinda train
you gonna drive?

When Gabe went back
to his mom,
Martha wiped her eyes.

I won't make you cry,
I told Martha,
'cause I'm never gonna leave.

Oh, honey,
Martha said,
the world's a big place.

Ruffin and Poker Face

I show Mom's photo to Mimi
and hold it up
next to my face.

Am I starting
to look like her
yet?

Ella, Mimi sighs,
you asked me that
last week.

Well, I grew
since then,
even my hair.
See.

My hair is so curly,
I have to pull it
out straight
from my head
for her to see.

You look like yourself, Ella.
A thousand gorgeous black curls,
great big blue eyes,
and eyelashes to die for,
Mimi says.

Are you taking Ruffin
with you
when you leave?
I ask her.
Ruffin is her betta fish.
He lives on her desk.

No, probably not.

We both watch Ruffin
swim around the roots
of the plant that grows
in his glass vase.

I'll take care of him
for you.
I'll talk to him,
like you do.
Hi there, Mr. Ruffin,
how's the water temperature
today?

I laugh 'cause I say it
just how Mimi did
when I spied on her.

Ruff-i-an,
she says,
not Ruffin.
His name is Ruffian.

I don't need
to go to college,
because I can already do
the job I want—
taking care of people's pets.

Everyone at Martha's
has a pet.
I have a calico cat,
Poker Face,
who sleeps on my bed.

I named her that
because Gabe said
poker face means
you can't tell
what someone is thinking.

Mimi's suitcase
is on the floor
in her room.
Before she goes to college,
she's going to
Camp To Belong.
It's where she gets to be
with her little brothers
for a week.

Camp To Belong
is on Salmon Lake
here in Maine.

It's only for foster kids
who have brothers or sisters
they don't get to live with.

They have a make-believe
birthday party,
where they give each other presents,
and they make a scrapbook
with photos of them
all together.

Mimi has two scrapbooks
already,
from the last two years,
and soon she'll have
three.
Her little brothers
live in Texas,
and she only sees them
the one week
out of the whole year.

I wish there was a camp
for kids and their pets.
I'd make
a scrapbook
with pet photos
and Poker Face
would be on the cover.

PART
TWO

PART
Two

A DOG NAMED STORM

I find my birthmother
and lose her
in the same second.

I have a sister named Ella
somewhere on this earth.
Where are you, Ella?
What are you like?
Do you know
about me?

Sunlight hits
the wood walls,
and it's like looking at
someone else's room.
Someone whose whole world
used to fit in a space
the size of R-Y-N-N.
Now there is "Sherry"
(who loved camping
and the ocean),
Ella, Uncle Curt Jr.,
and a set of (dead)
grandparents,
Yvette and Curt.

I don't tell Mom and Dad
about the flickering light
on Legacy.com,
but I print out the obituary
and hide it under my winter sweaters
in the bottom drawer
of my dresser
next to the photo
of Poster Boy.

I wonder what June and Terence
and Alexander will say
when I show them what I found.

It's almost too much
to think of meeting
my sister Ella
for the first time,
so I let myself imagine
the dog named Storm.

I bet he's a big dog
like a Lab or a German shepherd—
the kind that can sit up
in the front seat of a car,
and see out the window.

PICNIC

Me and June and Alexander
have a picnic for Douglas
with all his favorite foods
on a blanket in the backyard—
grape jelly sandwiches,
sweet melon slices,
juice boxes for everyone.

In between eating,
Douglas and I play catch
with his beach ball.
His eyes look straight at me
but his arms throw wild.
On a break from chasing the ball,
I stop to show June and Alexander
what I found on Legacy.com.

She's dead?
June stares at my phone
like it's impossible
a mom could be dead.

It's hard for me
to hear, too—
that I'll never see her
in this world,
that she won't see me.
It makes me

121

want to believe
I'll see her
in a heaven
where we meet
all the people
we miss.

June rubs her eyes.
I can't believe she died
before you even had a chance
to meet her, Rynn.

Why are you so sure
she's your birthmother?
Alexander asks.
Just because her name
was Scheherazade
and she'd be the right age?
What about
her daughter, Ella?

Now don't get all analytical
on us, Alexander,
June says,
handing him my phone,
take a closer look at her.

Alexander examines the photo
under the flickering candle.
I sit down on the blanket
and Douglas climbs in my lap.

He leans against me
and tips his juice box
to get the last drop.

My eyes are dry.
I look at the bits of clouds
left in the blue sky,
at the field of young corn,
at the laundry blowing
on Isabel's clothesline—
sock sock shirt shirt shirt
pants pants sock sock.

Hi, Mrs. Parkman,
I hear June say.

Mom stands in the yard.
The sunglasses on top
of her head
look up at the sky
the way I did.

Hello, June,
Mom answers,
but she watches me
and Douglas.
His head rests
on my shoulder,
and he plays with my hair.

I stopped at the farm stand

to get some garden tomatoes,
she shakes the plastic bag
she's holding,
*I thought I'd see where my daughter
is spending all her time these days.*

I'm Alexander, Douglas's brother,
Alexander waves to Mom,
*Douglas really likes Scheherazade.
She always makes things fun
for him.*

Does she?
Mom answers.
My feet are on the blanket
so there's no way to know
if the grass is heating up.
I can't tell if Mom stares
when Alexander says
Scheherazade,
because her sunglasses
are back on her face now—
two dark impenetrable disks.

*I'm glad she makes things fun
for someone,*
Mom says.

TOO MANY VOWELS

A hot wind blows
across my bare shoulders
as Mom turns to leave.
The corn in the field
bends back and forth.

Ouch, Alexander says,
when she's out of sight.
That was cruel.

She's probably having
a bad day,
I say.

I get that.
We all have bad days.
It's still cruel,
Alexander insists,
like he's the boy
in the "Emperor's New Clothes" story,
who can't help but report
exactly what he sees—
the only person who will say
the emperor is naked.

Deliberately cruel,
Alexander says,
as if he's decided

those are Mom's two words.
Couldn't she have said
Oh, hi there, Alexander,
heard you're visiting your dad,
how is the summer going?
Or, how about—
Your brother is very sweet.
I'm glad my daughter
makes things fun for him.

I notice Alexander says
brother, not half brother,
but I don't correct him.

You called me Scheherazade,
I explain.
Mom hates the name.
That's why they changed it.
Too many vowels.

June and Alexander
share a look.

Really?
June says.
That's the problem?
Too many vowels?

I've seen June's arguments
with her mom,
fights where the temperature

in the air
doesn't rise,
screaming that ends
in hugs instead of broken dishes.
Times when
I want to stare
and look away
at the same time.
Times where,
even though I know
my hole is fixed,
I feel the slosh
of my blood
losing its way
through my heart.

Does your Mom know?
Alexander asks.
Does she know
what you found out
about your birthmother?

No,
I answer.
Neither does my father.
He'd be interested
to hear what I learned
and he'd probably have ideas
on how to find her,
but I can't ask him
to keep it from Mom.

YELLOW JACKETS

Douglas climbs off my lap
to get a slice of melon.

Then he screams
and holds out his hand—
a buzz of angry yellow jackets
stinging and stinging and stinging him.

I was stung before,
when I stepped
on a yellow jacket nest
in the woods,
and I do what Dad did for me then—
grab Douglas
and race around the yard,
trying to escape the buzzing insects
and swatting at the ones
that chase after us.

Douglas thinks I invented
a new game called
Running in Circles,
and laughs then cries again,
when he feels the pain
of the stings.

When the yellow jackets fly off,
I stop to show Alexander and June

the red bumps on Douglas's hand.
We should put ice on it,
I tell them.

It's then I remember
Isabel asked for one thing—
to make sure
Douglas was safe.
Why did I think
that would be an easy promise
to keep?

There's no ice in the freezer,
so Douglas gets one Popsicle
for the stings on his hand,
and another to lick.

The screen door slams
and Isabel takes it all in.
Douglas's purple tongue
and orange hand—
both Popsicle-stained.

I thought I heard yelling
from the yard,
she says.

We were running from
yellow jackets,
I say.

June points to the Popsicles.
Douglas got stung.
We couldn't find ice,
but these seem to be
doing the job.

Isabel comes closer
and she frowns
at me.

But Rynn,
maybe you want me
to take you home now?

I feel the almost-cry
caught in my chest.

You don't want me back?
I didn't see the yellow jackets
before they stung him.
Really.

I know it would sound crazy
to say it wasn't my fault—
that they blew in
on the wind
that came
from Mom.

Isabel looks startled.

Why would you think that?

Of course I want you back.
It won't be the last time
he gets stung.
But look, you got stung, too, Rynn,
on your neck and shoulder.

Once she points it out,
I feel the pain
coming from the places
the yellow jackets landed
on me.
Alexander takes three Popsicles
from the freezer—
green and orange and purple—
and holds them out.

Are these for me to eat
or for my stings?
I ask.

Both,
he says,
and I take the green and the orange.

Toss me the purple,
June says to Alexander,
and catches it midair.
She tears off the wrapper
and makes a big show
of getting her tongue as purple
as Douglas's.

Thanks for inviting me
to your Popsicle party, little man,
she says to Douglas.
I wouldn't have missed it
for anything.

GIFTED

June's voice,
when she asked
that's the problem?
too many vowels?
was playful,
but her face was
completely serious.

There are things June knows
but doesn't bring up.

She knows I don't invite school friends
home.

It's more an exaggeration
than a lie
when I say the internet connection
at Garlic Farm
is too slow
for working on school projects,
or that Dad needs help
with his business.

She knows I don't talk
about Mom.

Because everyone loves moms
(isn't that what Mother's Day

is all about?)
so saying anything
would be like bad-mouthing
Santa.
And I think I'm also to blame—
the whole "it takes two to fight" thing—
although now I'm not sure
if that's true
if one of the two
is a child.

She knows her mom
kept my painting.

I made it at daycare—
a watercolor
of me and Mrs. Tibbetts
holding hands,
and underneath it said:

"I wisht I were your little girl."

Mrs. Tibbetts said she loved it
so much,
could she keep it herself
instead of hanging it up
with the other kids' pictures
for parents to see.

June knows I try hard.

Last year,
when Mom thanked her
for helping me with geometry,
telling June
to make me work for the answers
because those who aren't gifted
are always going to need
to try harder,
June said I did try hard
and she thought I was gifted
in my own way,
although Mom didn't ask
which way that was.

NAIL POLISH

After the day with the yellow jackets
I'm careful to stay out of Mom's way.

If she's inside,
and I hear the thud of her footsteps,
I'll head out
and push the wheel hoe
between rows of garlic—
Dad's trick to turn up weed seeds
before they have a chance to grow.

And even though I love Dad's meals,
sometimes I say I'm not hungry
and stay in my room
while Mom and Dad eat.

After they're in bed,
I go downstairs
to find a plate of food
Dad left for me
on the counter—
the mounds of pasta, carrots, and salad
not touching each other,
the way I liked it
when I was four.

I'm trying to learn a lesson—
not to get stung twice,

not to get knocked down
by the avalanche of molten rock
when it finally comes.

I used to try
being completely silent
when Mom was angry,
but that made things
worse.
Talking too much
could also backfire.

So I decide
the plan for now
is to only say
what is needed
and nothing more.

It's like Mom
also got a memo
about the new plan
for mother-daughter conversations,
because I'm in Dad's recliner
with my feet up
when she comes in
with her basket
of nail polishes.

Mani? Pedi?
What colors?

I pick a glittery red
and a flat white.

Red. White.
I tap my thumb
and then my pointer,
pause,
and say it again,
touching the other fingers,
Red. White.

Mom sits down on the floor
next to me.
Toes?
she asks.

Same,
I say.

Mom brushes on the colors
with careful but sure strokes.
I close my eyes,
feeling my hand
in hers.

After my heart surgery,
Mom did my nails
in the hospital.
I hurt so much I didn't care
what I looked like,
but it felt good

to have my hands held,
whatever the reason.

After my fingers are done
Mom drapes a towel
on the bottom
of the recliner
and starts in on my feet.

Well? she asks,
when she's finished.

Very nice,
I say.
Thank you.

Mom gets to her feet,
and stands back
while I wiggle my toes
and hold up my hands.

Not bad,
she says.

I agree,
I answer.

FARMERS MARKET

Some people are surprised
by all the varieties of garlic
at our booth.
It makes it hard to choose.

Can you recommend
a good baking garlic?
a woman asks me,
after standing there
for a while.

Music garlic
bakes up sweet,
I say.
You also can't go wrong
with German Extra Hardy,
and it keeps really well, too.

I'll get six of the Music garlic,
the woman decides.

We have a scale like Isabel's,
and I weigh them
and put them in a garlic bag.
The woman holds the bag
by its cloth ties
and strokes the fabric.

I've seen this happen
over and over
with Dad's bags—
something about them,
something more than fabric and thread,
gives people a dreamy look,
like they're remembering
a time they were
perfectly happy.

Before we leave,
I find Francine at her booth.
Today's cheese sample is
applewood-smoked ricotta.
First you taste the smoky,
then the apple comes through.

I need two more names
on a pumpkin.
One is Douglas.
D-O-U-G-L-A-S.
And the other is Ella.
E-L-L-A.

Will do,
Francine says,
and writes them down
on a paper napkin.

It's the first time
I feel like I really do have

a little sister,
one who might be sad
if she didn't get a name pumpkin, too.

DORMANT

Sometimes you forget
you live on a volcano island.
It looks like a grassy hill
or a purple mountaintop
touching the sky.

It's light out until late now,
and after work,
Mom lies on a lounge chair
in the backyard
with her eyes closed.

If you saw her
you'd think *peaceful*
or *perfect Maine summer*
or *soaking up the sun.*
You wouldn't think
could explode anytime.

An extinct volcano
is one that hasn't erupted
in ten thousand years,
and no one thinks
it will erupt again.

It's cut off
from its source of lava.

A dormant volcano
is different than extinct.
It's quiet now,
but could explode
at any time.

It's hard to know
for sure
whether a volcano
is extinct
or dormant,
unless you wait
ten thousand years.

I remind myself
how dangerous it is
to hope for extinct.

Then the blasts of lava,
the ash clouds
and red-hot rock fragments,
surprise you
in your sleep.

SOD SPECIALIST

My big attic bedroom
is command central
for missing persons research
and my bed
is ground zero.

I prop my iPad on a pillow
and type the name
of my birthmother's brother
from the obituary—
Curt Worthen Jr.

Three things come up.
One I've seen before, of course—
the obituary of
Scheherazade "Sherry" Worthen.

The second thing
is from Cops & Courts
from eight years ago.

And the third is the website of
Curt Evan Worthen Jr.,
sod and irrigation specialist,
Phoenix, Arizona.

At the top of the website
there's a photo
of a very green lawn

with a round pool
and a palm tree
in one corner.

Below it reads:

"The turf doctor
is ready to upgrade
your sun-scorched lawn
with clean, healthy sod
and create a backyard oasis.
For questions or to order,
please call."

There's a phone number
for Curt Evan Worthen Jr.'s business,
and I save it on my phone.

Then I print out the information
about Uncle Curt
and hide it with the other papers
in my sweater drawer.

The summer sky
outside my windows
finally turns dark,
but it's hard to fall asleep.
All I can think about
is the phone number.

I don't want to order sod,
but I do have questions.

PRESS ONE FOR EMERGENCY

Me and June,
and Alexander and Terence,
are on June's porch
that looks out on
the Tibbettses' big hay fields,
and at hills behind them
where Trues live.

Everyone wants to be there
when I call Uncle Curt.

Terence shaved his head,
and he rubs his hands
over his bare scalp.
I see a pale-pink splotch
of a birthmark
at the base of his neck
I never knew was there.

Why'd you do it, Terence?
I ask him.

Why not?
he answers.

What will your mom say?
I ask.

I did worse!
I did worse!
both June and Terence shout out.

Alexander looks puzzled.
He doesn't know
it's a pretty low bar
for June and her sisters and brother.
If they get a bad grade,
no problem.

I did worse.
I didn't even get a grade,
June's mom will say.

When Terence was learning
to drive, he went in reverse
instead of forward,
right through the back wall
of the garage.

I did worse,
June's mom told him,
describing the time
she totaled her dad's car
around a tree.

Why is your name Terence?
Alexander asks him.
Why didn't they give you a month
like your sisters

April, May, and June?
August would have been a good name
for a boy.

Terence scratches his bare head.
He looks like an underwater
sea creature,
with his bright-green eyes
and smooth scalp.

Why is a city boy here
in the middle of nowhere, Maine?
Terence asks Alexander.

Cut it out,
June play-slaps Terence
on the arm.

Sorry, Alexander,
she says,
you can see why Terence
didn't get to be a month.

I have to be here,
Alexander explains to Terence.
It's in my parents' agreement.
A week at Christmas,
and two weeks in the summer
until I turn sixteen,
which I will next month.
Then I get to decide

where I want to be
all year.

Terence looks surprised
by Alexander's honesty.

Cool, he answers,
good luck deciding.

Ask your uncle
what a turf doctor does,
Alexander suggests,
that would be a good
conversation starter.

Your sister is probably
living with him
in Arizona.
Maybe you'll get to
talk to her,
Terence says.

June filled him in on
Sherry and Ella.
Probably all the Trues
and Tibbettses know
by now.
I didn't say
to keep it secret—
it's been secret
long enough.

He's your uncle,
he's gonna be so excited
to hear from you.
I bet he'll want to fly you out there
to meet your sister,
you and a friend of your choice,
June predicts,
linking her arm in mine.

Everyone watches me look
at my phone.

Don't think,
just do it,
Terence says,
something he must have learned
from shaving off all his hair.

So I do.

The phone rings once,
and I turn it on speakerphone

Then it rings three more times
and a recording says,

You've reached Curt Worthen,
Phoenix's finest turf specialist.
Sorry I can't answer right now.
I'm either on another call
or out in the field.

If this is an emergency,
press one to leave your number
and I'll get right back to you,
or stay on the line to leave
a message.

I try to imagine
the kind of emergency
a person would press one for—
turf that turned brown overnight,
or an irrigation system
that won't shut off?

My attic research taught me
Phoenix gets the most sunshine
of any big city in the US—
three hundred days of sun
a year.
Does Ella walk across a green lawn
to go swimming in a round pool?

June is waving at me
to do something,
when the line goes dead.

I stare at the phone.
It's the first time
I've heard the voice
of someone from my home planet.

It's like their spaceship

finally landed here on earth,
and if I press one
or stay on the line,
I can communicate with them.

Do you want ME
to leave a message?
Terence asks.
I could say our lawn
was wrecked by moles,
and does he deliver
brand-new lawns
to Maine.

Very funny, Terence,
June says,
rapping her knuckles
on his bare head.

I redial one, two,
three, four, five,
six, seven
times.

I don't press one
for emergencies,
or leave a message.

Instead, I listen to the voice
of Uncle Curt,
saying the same thing

over and over and over,
until the eighth time,
when a woman's voice says
something new,
The mailbox is full.
Please try again
another time.

No one says anything
about my listening
to the recording
over and over and over
and staring at my phone.

If you want a job
while you're here,
Terence tells Alexander,
Dad and I are splitting firewood
to sell this fall.

You work with your dad?
With a wood splitter?
There's something wistful
in Alexander's voice.

Yeah, it's hot, dirty work,
and noisy, too.
We don't do it the way
Rynn's dad does.

Terence lifts both arms

up in the air
like he's holding an
imaginary ax,
slams them down,
and then up and down
one more time.

Whew,
he blows out his breath,
two chunks of wood—
should heat us
for at least an hour.

You tell your dad,
Terence says to me,
if he ever gets tired
of doing it
the old-timey way,
we'll come over
with the splitter,
and do all his wood
for the year
in a day.

I might like working
with you and your dad,
Alexander says to Terence.
He rubs his right thumb
across the two fingers
with the circles.

Well, let me know.
We could use the help.
And my hair,
Terence smooths his scalp
with his hands,
like his blond curls
are still there,
I got tired of picking ticks
out of it.
There's lots of ticks
in the woodyard.

I see Alexander is thinking
about it all—
working with Terence
and his dad,
the wood splitter,
ticks—
the same way I'm thinking
about pressing one
for emergency—
wanting it
and afraid of it
at the same time.

WE NEVER KNEW ABOUT YOU

I wait to call again
until I'm home.
It's almost dark out,
and I sit on the stone bench
behind the garlic garden.
I'm shaking so hard,
even my teeth chatter.

Uncle Curt's voice is back,
and this time
I press one.

Hi,
a woman answers,
Kissy Worthen speaking.
How can I help you?

All I can think is
Kissy?
Really?
but I speak before the words
freeze in my throat.

Can I talk to Curt Evan Worthen Jr.?

This is his wife.
What's your emergency?

I take a deep breath
before I speak.

*I don't really have
a sod emergency.
I saw the online obituary
of Scheherazade Worthen
and I think your husband
is my uncle.*

At first, there's no sound
from the phone.

Sorella? Is this Ella calling?

*No, I'm not Ella.
I thought Ella lived with you.*

Then who are you?
she asks.

*I'm Sherry's daughter, too.
I'm sixteen, and she gave me up
for adoption after I was born.*

*Sixteen?
Curt was in the service
sixteen years ago,
and was out of touch
with his family,*
Kissy says.
Are you sure

Sherry was your mother?
We never knew about you.

When she says
we never knew about you,
I lie back on the bench
and look up at the orange sunset.
Even in the heat,
the speckled stone
is cool beneath me.

A gray squirrel runs up the trunk
of a tree, stops for a second,
then runs back down
the way it came
and is gone into the woods.
When it stopped on the tree,
I could see its squirrel heart beating
through its skin.

I know that no one
can erase your life
with one sentence,
but that's what it feels like.

Instead of answering Kissy's question,
I ask one of my own.

Where is Ella, then,
and why did you call her
Sorella?

Sorella is her full name.
She doesn't live with us.
There were things in the past,
things Curt had to deal with,
that made it impossible.
Then he moved out here
and started the business.
We have two little boys
now, twins.

I have an idea
what she means about *things*,
because the second *thing* I saw online
about Curt Evan Worthen Jr.
was how he'd been arrested
for "unlawful possession
of scheduled drugs."

If Sorella/Ella is not
swimming in a round pool
in the desert of Phoenix,
where is she?

I hear a beep,
and Kissy Worthen says
she has another emergency call
coming in.

Where do you live?
she asks me.

Maine.

Maybe we can FaceTime
with you soon.
I'll talk to Curt.
This is all very sudden.

Okay,
I say.
I don't ask what's so *sudden*—
my emergency phone call
that wasn't an emergency
or me.

When I hang up, I google
S-O-R-E-L-L-A.

Sorella
(seven letters,
three vowels, one repeat)
is "a feminine noun
that means *sister* or *sibling*
in Italian."

There's a list of ways
to use the word.
Mia sorella.
My sister.

Grande sorella.
Big sister.

Sorella minore.
Younger sister.

Ciao, sorella.
Hello, sister.

My birthmother also gave
her second child
a name with a clue—
that even if I wasn't there
with Ella,
she was a sister.

Sorella

Gravy

Ella, honey,
Martha says,
why don't you take Gravy
outside.
You don't need to watch me
huffing and puffing
on the treadmill.

Martha is wearing
new sneakers
that are bright white.

I'm watching to see
if you'll suddenly go fast,
like Hocus and Pocus.

Martha has to walk
on the treadmill
every day now
for exercise
and she hates exercise.

Gabe's mice
Hocus and Pocus
ran fast
on the wheel

in their cage,
making it go
around and around.
Martha is only walking.

Gravy is Martha's pet.
He's a dog,
and Martha says in people years
he's older than she is,
which is a lot.
Gravy is brown and short haired
and he likes water
and chewing on sticks.

Gabe took Hocus and Pocus
with him when he left.

Please take Gravy outside.
Rest easy, I'm only going
one speed on this thing.

I don't mind
taking Gravy for walks.
He likes me second best
next to Martha,
'cause I find sticks
for him to chew.

Before we go outside
I check on Ruffin.
I wiggle his plant

to make waves
so he'll feel like
he's in a real pond.

Gravy goes pee,
and I spy on Martha
through the back window.
She told the truth.
Her white sneakers
aren't going any faster.

There's a house
up the block
where no one lives.
In the front yard
branches from a big tree
are all over the lawn.

I find a stick that's as long
as Gravy.
He carries it in his mouth
the whole way home.
He can breathe
and hold a stick
between his teeth.
I tried and I couldn't do it
for even a minute.

Pet Plants

When I first met Roshni
I asked her
if she had any pets.
She said her plants
are her pets.

Sorry, but I don't think plants
can be pets,
I said.

Then she said they're living things
and she has to water them
and give them plant food.

It seemed like she really wanted
me to believe they were pets.
So now when she visits
I always ask her,
How are your plants?

Today Roshni says,
I hear Mimi is going away
to college.
How are you feeling about that?

I might get her room,
I answer.

You and Mimi have been together
with Martha for a while,
she says.

Yes, and I'm going to feed her betta fish
when she's gone,
I say.
But why do you want to talk
all about Mimi?
I thought you came here
to see me.

I did come to see you.
But I thought you might want to talk
about Mimi going away.
I know you were sad
when Gabe left.

Well, I don't,
I explain.
How are your plants?

Rynn

POMPEII

Small earthquakes were felt
for four days
before the eruption
of Mount Vesuvius
in AD 79,
but no one knew
they were warnings
of what was to come—
columns of volcanic gas
so tall they blocked the sun,
firestorms of stones and ash
that incinerated or suffocated
everything in its path.

If someone had told
the people of Pompeii
the mountain they saw every day
was about to blow its top,
would they have believed it?

Would they have left
without looking back?

Mom is in the doorway
of my room.
I quickly close
my bottom dresser drawer.

It's filling up
with the pile of papers
I printed.
One day I want to make
a poster collage—
of all the new family
I find.

I have so much to think about,
I don't pay attention
to the way Mom taps
her wedding ring
on the doorframe
when she talks,
making little vibrations.

Kissy Worthen followed me
on Instagram,
and I followed her back.
Now I have pictures
of my twin cousins,
Brayden and Kaden,
playing outside with a little dog.
I was surprised
their backyard has no turf
at all, no green oasis—
it's cement with patio furniture,
a fire pit, and an egg-shaped pool.

There are photos of Uncle Curt
where he looks much happier
than on Cops & Courts.

He's stretched out
on a lawn chair
under a blue umbrella.
His second toe is longer
than his big toe,
just like mine,
and his hair is reddish brown.

Aunt Kissy texted
that she and Uncle Curt
want to FaceTime
when I'm ready.

Supper is in ten minutes,
Mom says.

Even upstairs,
I can smell Dad's
yeasty challah bread,
fresh from the oven.

Okay, I'll be right down,
I say.

Mom's foot thumps impatiently
on the wood floor
before she turns to leave,
but I'm thinking about
where to start looking
for Ella,
and what it would feel like
to find her.

BAD BUG

Douglas's pink sting marks
are gone,
but whenever he sees
anything flying
in the air,
he hits out at it
with both hands
and yells,
BAD BUG.

Black flies and mosquitoes,
even ladybugs and dragonflies
are *BAD BUGS* now.
Douglas is sure
they're all out to hurt him.
I join in,
waiting for my own chance
to see a bug before he does.

BIG BAD BUG,
I yell,
flapping my arms
when a blue jay
flies across the yard.

No, Win,
Douglas gives me a strange look,
dats a bird.

THE SPITTING IMAGE

Kissy texts that
it's two hours earlier
in Phoenix, Arizona.
That's a time zone thing
I never understood—
like how it can be summer
in one place
and winter in another
on our same planet.
If I lived long ago,
I'd be one of those people
who thought the world
was flat,
and the sun rotated
around the earth.

We're going to FaceTime
at ten o'clock their time,
which is twelve o'clock
my time.

Mom is at work
and Dad is in his sewing room.

I sit on the rug
next to my bed.
My phone rings
and faces come into view.

They're both outside
next to their pool.
Aunt Kissy is wrapped
in a pink octopus-print towel.

Uncle Curt
stares at me,
and his mouth actually
hangs open,

My God,
you're the spitting image.

He's so far away
in his time zone,
and also right there
turning his head
to study me
like I'm an animal
in a zoo.
I think about making
chimp noises.

I do? I do?
I look like her?
My face, my hair?

It's the first time in my life
anyone ever said I looked like
someone else.

Oh, yes, everything,
Uncle Curt says,
still staring,
and Aunt Kissy
kisses his cheek,
then kisses the tips
of her own fingers
and waves them toward me.

I'm starting to figure out
how she got her name.

Uncle Curt is still staring.
I think about hopping up and down
or stuffing food in my face,
or walking my hands up
an invisible glass wall.

What should we call you?
Kissy asks.

My parents changed my name
to Rynn,
but you can call me Scheherazade,
I say, the same way I told
Alexander.
Actually, do you know
how my birthmother
got her name?
I don't know anyone else
named Scheherazade.

I think my mother read the name
in some book,
and thought it was pretty.
She didn't consider how much fun
it would be for a kid to spell.
So, Scheherazade,
Uncle Curt says
from his time zone
to mine,
what are your other questions for us?

My first question
is easy.

Where is Ella?

Uncle Curt looks down
at his white swim shorts.
His legs are very tanned,
probably from the three hundred days
of sunshine.
I don't know.
After Sherry passed away,
the state contacted Ella's father,
Rob Buzzell.
He and Sherry had split up.
Ella was with Rob
for a while
but then he went to jail,
and she went into foster care.
I wasn't in a position

to take her.

I don't mention what I read about his
"unlawful possession of
scheduled drugs."

The next question
pops out of my mouth,
What about MY birthfather?
Do you know who he is?

Even if he was "not involved,"
maybe Uncle Curt knows
his name.

He shakes his head,
I'm sorry.
I have no idea.
I was overseas then.

The third question is one
Mom and Dad never knew
the answer to, so I ask,
Why did my mother want me
to grow up on a farm?

That's an easy one,
Uncle Curt nods.
When we were growing up,
Sherry and I had the best times
on our grandparents' farm.

She loved swimming in the pond,
picking blackberries,
and playing with the bunnies
and the goats.

It's hard to get the words out
for my next question.

Sorry, I couldn't hear you,
Uncle Curt leans forward,
so I have to say it again.

How did my mother die?

I think I can guess
what happened.
She had a hole
somewhere in her body
no one knew about
for a long time,
like mine in my heart.
Maybe hers was in her lungs,
and one day
she went to take a breath,
and there was no air left.
Or it could have been
an overdose.
June's sister April
almost died two times.
Now she drives to Bangor
every morning,

to get methadone
at the clinic.

Uncle Curt looks off
toward their pool
when he tells me.

It was a crazy thing.
She died from the flu.
Apparently, it still happens
in this day and age.
Perfectly healthy people
dying from the flu.

His face gets fuzzy,
and I press my eyes
to stop the tears.

This is a lot to take in at once,
Scheherazade,
Aunt Kissy says,
let's talk again soon
and you can meet
your cousins.
Brayden's got your same
dark-gray eyes.

She does the finger-kissing thing
again, and so does Uncle Curt
(she probably taught him how),
and I do it back to them—

kiss kiss the ends of my fingers
and hold them out at my phone
as we all say goodbye.

BIG HEART

My doctors said
a big heart is a bad thing.
They fixed my hole
to keep my heart
from growing.
With hearts,
bigger is not better.
It means your heart
has to work harder
to pump your blood
all through your body.

Your heart is as big as this,
a doctor once told me,
folding my fingers
into a tight little ball.
That made me think
my heart was small and hard,
and ready to fight.

But now,
it feels like my heart
is unclenching its fist.

It started with Douglas,
and how he thinks
everything I do
is perfect.

Then I found out about Ella,
and all the love
I didn't know I had,
I have.

I want to give everyone
a personalized pumpkin—
sweet Douglas,
my sister, Ella,
wherever she is,
Isabel and Big Doug,
Terence and June,
April and May,
analytic Alexander,
my new cousins, Brayden and Kaden,
my finger-kissing aunt and uncle,
Mom and Dad
and even people
I never met.

NO PLACE TO GO

On our way back
from the Saturday farmers market,
Dad and I eat leftover slices
of Vincent and Hugh's
pizza of the day
(portabella mushrooms,
red peppers, arugula)
and we sing
our garlic song—
the one dad made up
many years ago
to entertain me
on the ride home
from the market.

Oh, all through the winter,
the garlic is waiting,
waiting to grow.

Oh, all through the winter,
the garlic is shiv'ring,
under the snow.

All in a row,
deep under the snow,
waiting to grow,
OH!

When we get home
Dad unloads the table
and the unsold boxes
of garlic and garlic vinegar,
and I head inside
with my unclenched heart,
still singing.

Then I notice the radio is on loud
in the kitchen,
much too loud—
almost drowning out the vacuum cleaner
that sounds like it's banging against the walls
of the living room
like a Roomba gone wild.
Except we don't have a Roomba.

I stop singing.
This would be the time to leave.
When I was younger
and heard cupboard doors slamming
or chairs knocked over,
I would have known to hide.
But today I'm not just Rynn,
I'm also Scheherazade,
and I walk forward
instead of backward.

When Mom sees me
in the doorway of the living room,
she stomps on the off switch

of the vacuum cleaner.
The radio is still blaring.

Were you ever going to tell me?
She says the words so slowly
I wonder if maybe I could try
and only count every other one, like
Were. Ever. To. Me?

Tell you what?
I ask.

*Or did you just tell
all your friends?*

Or. You. Tell. Your.

She takes a pile of papers
off the coffee table behind her
and shakes them at me.
It's the pictures
of Poster Boy,
Uncle Curt wearing orange,
and the flickering candle
that tells about the grandparents
and birthmother
I never got to know.
And it's all the photos
of Brayden and Kaden and Kissy
smiling and waving at me
from Phoenix, Arizona.

I knew you were hiding something,
she says.

I. You. Hiding.

*Did you see
my birthmother is dead,
and my sister is gone?*
I say.

I reach for the papers
but Mom won't let go.
She yanks them back
and I grab the edges
in a tug-of-war,
until they rip apart,
pieces falling everywhere.
Mom drops the shreds left
in her hand.

*You think these people
care about you?*

I get down on the rug
and start crawling around,
gathering up the ripped papers
and stuffing them in my pockets.
I see a sliver
of Poster Boy's face—
part of one eye
and a corner of his mouth.

Mom's hand clamps tight
around my arm,
and she tries to pull me up
off the floor.
I feel the sharp tips
of her nails.

I twist my arm free
and run upstairs.
My heart thumps twice
THUD THUD
like it's trying to restart.

In Pompeii—
the people who survived
the first day of the eruption
were killed by superheated gases
the next day.

In my room,
I hardly know
what I'm putting
in my backpack.
Before I leave,
I stop for a second
and bury my face
in the sky-blue curtains
Dad made.

Then I go in Mom and Dad's room,
and take the photos Mom keeps

in the bottom
of her jewelry box—
the ones she doesn't know
I know are there.

When I come downstairs,
the radio is off
and Mom has her back to me.
I put the ultrasound prints
on the coffee table.

I would never hurt
your lost babies,
I say to her
very quietly.

It's true.
I feel sorry for Mom's
blurry gray children,
with their black dot eyes
and their curled-up bodies,
who never got
to breathe air.

Mom turns around
and bursts into tears,
just as Dad comes in.

Leanne? Rynn?
I hear Dad's two words echoing
in the house

as the door bangs shut
behind me.

I run past the garden,
where the spire-shaped bulbs
and curlicue stems
of a few garlic scapes
are still growing.

My heart is suddenly beating hard,
BOOMPA BOOMPA BOOMPA,
like it wants to beat itself
out of my chest.
I push back against it
with my hand.

I put on my backpack
and ride my bike
down the driveway
and onto the road.

When I was younger
and the earth shook,
I climbed into
the tree house Dad built.
I thought no one
could find me there.

Or I hid
from the heat
under the back porch.

The ground felt like
a person's cool hand
against my face.

In the winter,
I pulled the covers
over my head,
or looked at my blue curtains
and imagined they were
a faraway sky.

Every story about little kids
packing a suitcase
and running away from home
ends with laughter,
hot cocoa, and hugs.

It's really not funny at all
that when you're little,
there's no place else
to go
but the same home
you just left.

ESCAPE

Terence says cars have
blind spots—
places that can't be seen
when you look ahead
or through the side mirrors.

Something could be right next to you,
and you wouldn't see it
unless you turned your head.

Dad might have a blind spot
for Mom—
she's so close to him,
he can't always see
what she's doing—
and he doesn't bother
to turn his head.
If that's what it means by
love is blind
I don't want
that kind of love.

I'm not sure
if there are blind spots
on bicycles,
but I only look
straight ahead.

All I feel is the hot summer wind,
my heart working hard on the hills,
and the weight of my backpack.

I don't have a plan
for where I'm going,
but when I get to
Isabel's driveway,
Alexander is on the front lawn,
as if I'd wished him
there.

Scheherazade,
on her bicycle
with a backpack,
he calls out.

I lean the bike
against a wooden fence
and sit down
in the grass.

I try to steady
my voice,

Alexander,
here on the farm
six more days.

He walks toward me,
in a T-shirt and shorts.

No pressed pants
and dress shirt.

Actually,
Alexander grins,
looking like Douglas
for just a second,
I'm here for the rest
of the summer.
I'm gonna work with
Terence and his dad
on firewood.
And get this—
when I asked,
my mom said it's about time
I learn what it means
to earn my own money.
And of course,
I can move all the wood I want,
as long as I don't use
the splitter.

I try to smile back
at Alexander,
but my lips won't move
in the right shape.

Alexander looks at me more
closely,
and his expression changes.
He comes over
and kneels down

in the grass
in front of me.

You're shaking,
Scheherazade.
Your whole body
is shaking.
What happened?

I feel for the shredded papers
in my jean shorts pockets,
the ones I collected
off the floor.
I show him
all the pieces.

It was bad.
My people
got torn up.

Alexander gently takes
the wadded clumps
from me.

Oh, they did?
he says,
in the same voice I use with Douglas
when I can't understand
what he's saying,
but I want him to know
I'm still interested.

Scheherazade,
where are you going
on your bike?

I don't know,
I answer.

I want to ask him
if he believes in curses,
if people are born
deliberately cruel
or does something happen
to make them that way,
if the only spells
you can break
are your own,
if it's better to run from danger
or face it,
and would you even know
if you had a blind spot.

But my teeth are chattering
so hard,
I can't begin to speak.

Do you want to stay for supper?
Isabel made mac and cheese,
the kind with crunchy bread-crumb topping.
And for dessert, your favorite—
Popsicles.
I give him a thumbs-up,
and Alexander puts his hand out

to help me up.

If you're down a well,
someone could throw you
a rope.
If you're in a nosediving plane,
and there's a parachute,
you could jump free.
If you're on the second floor
of a burning house,
you could climb down
the fireman's ladder
or leap into a net.

So many ways to escape.
Alexander's hand in mine
feels like
a rope,
a parachute,
a ladder,
and a net
all at once.

I follow Alexander into the kitchen,
where the big farm table
is set for supper.

Look who was riding by.
Scheherazade!
So I invited her for supper,
Alexander says.

Douglas stands up
in his chair
and claps his hands,
Win sit wit me.

Big Doug takes a fifth plate
and silverware from the cupboards
as if it's that easy
to welcome another person.

Rynn,
Isabel says,
what a great surprise.
Are you okay?
You seem a little
out of breath.

I'm okay,
I say,
I rode my bike fast
up the hills.

The casserole on the table,
smells so good and cheesy.
There's also a jar
of Isabel's pickles.

Wow, this all looks delicious,
I say, and take a seat
between Douglas and
Alexander.

I kick my sandals off
under the table.
As always, the wooden floorboards
are solid and cool
against the bottoms
of my feet.

Alexander serves me first,
like I'm a special guest.
I get a big corner piece
of mac and cheese,
and it's the best.

Pick-ul,
Douglas fishes a pickle
from the jar.
He twists it in half
and gives the two pieces
to me and Alexander.
Pickle juice drips
from his hands.

Nice sharing, Douglas,
Alexander says,
eating his half.

Thank you, Douglas,
very yummy,
I say.

Sometime between mac and cheese

and pickle,
my shaking stops.
The breezes that come through
the open windows are cool,
the way they are
at the end of a summer day.

After supper,
Alexander walks outside
with me.

I have to go,
I say.

What can I do?
he asks.

You already did it,
I say.
But I wanted to ask you
one thing before I leave.
Remember you said cruel,
deliberately cruel,
about my mom.
What do you think
makes someone like that?

I'm not sure,
Alexander answers seriously,
as if it's a normal question
to ask someone

on a driveway
outside a farm
while the moon slowly rises.
Maybe something is missing.

Okay, thanks,
I say, as if he's given me
the analytical answer
to an algebra problem.
I can understand that—.
I've had parts of myself
go missing, too.

At the end of the driveway,
I only hesitate a second,
before turning my bike right
down the hill,
instead of left
toward home.

HURRY

I don't get far—
only around the curve
past the big barn
and greenhouses
on the farm,
when I feel a sharp pain
in my chest.
My heart speeds up
like a fist pounding and pounding
on a door.

I don't know
what will happen
if it keeps beating
this fast.
If the hole they fixed
will open again,
the way Dad
pulls out a seam,
one little stitch
at a time,
until nothing
is holding the cloth
together.

I drop my bike
in the road,
and get my phone

out of the front
of my backpack.
June's home number,
the one I called
all the years
before we both
got cell phones,
is the one
I dial.
My lips
are tingling.
June's mom answers
on the second ring.

Mrs. Tibbetts,
something's wrong
with me.
My heart's beating
really fast
and it's hard
to breathe.
Can you come
get me?

Where are you, Rynn?
she asks.

On the road
past Douglas's house,
I think I need to go
to the hospital.

Stay right there,
I'm on my way,
she says.

I sit in the gravel
on the side of the road,
and press my hands hard
against the ribs
over my heart.
I wonder if this is how
I'll die.
All by myself,
looking out on
fields of corn and wheat,
with the sun going down
over the hill.

If I die now,
I'll never meet
my sister, Ella,
my twin cousins
in Arizona,
or get to show Douglas
how to play
hide-and-seek.
And I won't see Alexander
any more days.

Mrs. Tibbetts's car pulls up,
and she's by my side
in a second.

Her June-green eyes
are wide.

Rynn, what's happening?
Did you take something?
You can tell me.

I know June's sister April
scared her mother
too many times.

No, Mrs. Tibbetts,
it's not that.
My heart is beating
really fast
and I'm dizzy.

In the car
I tell my lungs,
Breathe
Breathe.

What about your parents,
do they know what's happening?
Mrs. Tibbetts asks.

No,
I say,
and she looks over at me quickly,
then back at the road.

Please hurry,
I'm really scared,
I beg.

And she does.

CAVE WOMAN

My hard breathing
and my thumping heart
get me a bed
in the emergency room
behind a curtain
that hangs all the way
from the ceiling
to the floor.

It's not the big hospital
in Portland
that fixed my holes,
but it smells the same.

I'm glad to be in a place
where they know how
to keep people alive,
and how to bring them back
to this world
when they die.

A nurse with "Laila RN"
on her name badge
gives me a hospital gown
to put on,
open in the front, please,
then gives me privacy
to put it on

behind the curtain.
She does all the things
I've had done before—
sticky round pads on my chest
and belly,
wires attached to the pads.

I'm still shaking
and she covers me
with warm blankets.

That's one of my names, too—
Rynn,
I say,
pointing to her badge,
but she doesn't get it.

I watch my heartbeat
on the monitor—
122 124 124 126 123.
Mrs. Tibbetts sits in a chair
next to my bed
and strokes my head.

Are you taking any medications?
my name twin Laila RN asks.

I take gummy-bear vitamins,
mostly the red ones.

Her eyebrows shoot up,
and she types something

into the computer.

You're her mother?
Laila asks Mrs. Tibbetts,
who shakes her head no,
and gets up.

I think her parents
were notified.
I'll go give them
another call,
she says,
and leaves the room.
My heart speeds up
on the monitor—
132 135 133 135 134.

They take blood
from my arm,
and cover the spot
with a Band-Aid.

Laila introduces "N. Aden PA."
He says he's a physician's assistant.
His skin is dark brown
and his hand reaches out
to shake mine,
like we're at a party.
Then he sits down
on a little stool
with wheels.

He says he read about
my surgeries
in my record.
Very, very interesting,
he says,
like my record
was a good book
and I should read it, too,
when I had the chance.

He asks me about
the tingling,
the hard breathing,
my fast heart,
the dizziness.

Am I dying?
I ask him.
*Did my heart defect open up
again?
Or do I have another hole
somewhere?*

PA makes a sad face
and wheels himself
right up to me.
I can see his nose hairs.

*Your oxygen level is good,
and your monitor strip,
except for the elevated heart rate,*

is reassuring.
I understand this came on
suddenly.
May I ask what was happening
when it started?

I stare at him,
and do an eyebrow raise
like Laila.
What can I say?
That I was running away
but didn't get very far.
I ignore his question
and ask him one of my own.

If everything is fine,
then what's wrong
with my heart?

I don't know what they teach
in PA school,
so I point to the monitor
to show him what I mean.

PA looks up at the monitor,
then back at me.

Rynn, we think what you're experiencing
is a panic attack.
It can feel like you're dying,
make your heart rate increase,

and affect your breathing.
It's real.
And we can give you something
to help with the symptoms.

When he's done with his speech,
Laila comes to the bed
with water and a round pill
in a clear plastic cup,
like they'd already planned it,
talking about me
on the other side
of my curtain.

It's what's called fight-or-flight,
a very primitive human response,
PA adds.
Your body thinks something is dangerous
or life threatening,
and prepares to defend itself.
It probably helped cave people survive.

After I swallow the little pill,
I lie there
under the blankets
like a cave woman,
and wait for the worst
to be over.

SPELL

The heavy hospital door
clicks open
and wakes me up.

Someone turned off the lights
in the room,
but the green numbers
next to the red heart
on the monitor
read 68 72 64 67.

Mrs. Tibbetts is sitting in the chair
next to me,
wide awake,
her feet up on my bed.
She watches the monitor, too.

Laila RN pulls the curtain,
and Dad is there
in his garden jeans
holding a garlic bag.

When Dad's in a hospital,
he looks like a person
who time traveled there
from the past.

Maybe because when he was

growing up,
he never went to a hospital.
Instead, when he was sick
the doctor came to the apartment
and gave him a shot
with a long needle.

Dad had diseases
people get vaccines for now—
measles, mumps, and chicken pox,
and even an old-fashioned one
called scarlet fever.

He told me stories
about what it was like.

They kept me in a dark room
until my fever broke.

They tied mittens on my hands
so I couldn't scratch.

Laila takes the blood pressure cuff
off my arm,
and disconnects the monitor.

They said your little spell
is over, and your heart is fine,
Dad says to me.
Nothing to worry about.

I don't answer
because I'm thinking
about what Dad just said.
If it's true,
who put the spell
on me?

BREAD CRUMBS

Is Leanne here?
Mrs. Tibbetts asks.

She's home
with a terrible migraine,
Dad says.

Mrs. Tibbetts puts her hand
on my arm,
and Dad sets the garlic bag
on the bedside table.

I brought you a snack.
Some leftover challah,
he says,
like I'm in first grade
and forgot my lunch.
I have the van out front.
They said you can leave anytime.

NO, NO,
my two words
come out loud and deep,
the way I imagine
they would sound
in a cave,
echoing off rock walls.
They sound so good

I say them again,
NO, NO,
I'm going back with Mrs. Tibbetts,
and staying with June for a while.

Dad scratches his head.
His faded blue eyes look
from me to Mrs. Tibbetts.

Sure thing,
she says, as if we'd
already discussed it,
June won't say so
but she misses having her sisters
around,
and Rynn always brings out the best
in my wild boy Terence.

Then she gives Dad her
"I did worse."
I spent my whole junior year
at my Grammie True's.

Pick me up next Saturday morning
for farmers market?
I ask Dad.

His face lights up.

Of course!
he agrees.

When Mrs. Tibbetts and I
leave the hospital,
it's dark out.
She yawns
and rubs her eyes.

During the school year,
she's a crossing guard,
and when school lets out,
she works for a paving company
as a flagger—
the person who stands on the road
in a fluorescent orange vest
and tells cars when to stop
and when to go.

In Mrs. Tibbetts's summer job,
she's outside
all day
in the heat,
breathing in the smell
of fresh asphalt.

I'm sorry, I say,
for keeping you up late.

Not to worry, Rynn,
she says,
I'm just glad you're okay.
Stay with us

as long as you want,
no questions asked.

Why did you go live
with your Grammie True
your junior year?
I ask.

I'm not sure.
I stayed there one night,
and then another,
and it ended up being a year.
You know how good a cook she is,
and she'd make all my favorites.
It's not like I didn't see my family.
They were right down the road.
I guess I liked her fussing over me.

Did she make you her
chocolate cream pie?

Oh, yes,
Mrs. Tibbetts says.

On the way to Beacon,
I eat pieces
of Dad's challah,
and also throw crumbs
out the open car window.
There's a fairy tale

where kids drop bread crumbs.
I can't remember
how it worked—
if it was for their family
to track them down,
or for them
to find their way
home again.

When we get
to the house
June and Terence
are waiting up.

Mom called to let us know
where she was,
and that you were okay,
June hugs me.

Alexander couldn't reach you,
so he texted me.
I told him you were
coming back here
with Mom,
Terence says.

I turned off my phone
in the hospital,
I say.

There are two beds

in June's room—
her bed and May's old bed.
There's probably a Rynn-shaped sag
in May's mattress
from a thousand sleepovers.

Before I left home,
I stuffed my backpack
like a four-year-old—
bathing suit, red dress,
panda slippers, sweatshirt,
hair ties, and a tank top
but no toothbrush,
no hairbrush,
and no underwear.

I also don't have pajamas
in my backpack,
but I find a soft T-shirt
to wear.

I stretch out on May's bed
and listen to the sound
of dishes clattering,
water running,
and Tibbettses talking
in low voices.

Before we left the hospital,
I asked one more time,
just to be sure.

PA was very serious
when he answered,

Your heart is fine, Rynn,
and there's no reason to think
you have any other defects.

Then he answered the other question
I asked,
when we were alone,

There's also nothing in your chart
or in medical literature
that suggests your birth defects
were your birthmother's fault.
We're complex creatures
and sometimes things go wrong
without any explanation.

June's room has fairy lights
strung where the walls
meet the ceiling.
They shine like hundreds
of little stars
above me.

I turn on my phone.
Nothing from Mom,
but there are six missed calls
and messages
from Alexander

and a text from Kissy.

I hold my hand
over my *fine* heart
when I read what Kissy says:

"Just fyi—Curt called the state
to ask if they knew where Ella was
and to tell them about YOU.
Fingers crossed!
XOXO"

EXILE

The word *exile*
means you can't go back
to the place
you came from.
Does the *X* in *exile*
mark the spot
where you are now,
or where you once lived?

It's not really X-ile
at June's house,
but it's not home, either.

After a volcano erupts,
the molten lava flows
over the ground,
then cools into solid rock,
changing the landscape
forever.

When I wake up
in June's room
the next morning,
her bed is empty.
I'm still wearing
the red plastic bracelet
the hospital gave me,
because I'm allergic
to penicillin.

I take a hot shower
and wash away
the hospital smell,
and the sticky stuff
left on my skin
from the monitor pads.
I braid my wet hair
and brush my teeth
with my finger.

I could go back home
and get more of my things,
but the hardest part
was leaving,
and I don't want
to have to leave
again.

June and Terence
are in the kitchen,
eating cereal and milk.
I pour cereal into a bowl.
It's like a regular sleepover,
but it's not.

*You've got a lot
of names,*
Terence pushes the milk
across the table to me.
*You're Rynn,
Alexander calls you
Scheherazade,*

and June said Douglas
calls you Win.

That's true,
I agree,
so which one are YOU going
to call me?

I fall right into Terence's
trap.

I've got my own name
for you.
Terence points his spoon
at me.
My new sister July,
and he's so pleased with himself,
I can't help but laugh.

OVALS

Through June's kitchen window
we watch Alexander ride up
on my bike.

Mom asked him
to get it off the road,
June explains.

People talked about me
while I was in my hospital cave.
I'm thinking all the Tibbetts and Trues
know where I was
last night.
I don't really mind.
It almost makes me
one of them,
for my business
to be everyone else's business
too.

I go out to meet him.

Alexander,
riding my bike
in Beacon, Maine.

You're okay now?
he asks.
He's wearing a tan brimmed hat

that looks like one of Terence's.

Yes, my heart is all good,
I tap my line.

Alexander leans the bike
against the house.

I figured that out—
how your heart
was all good—
the first time I met you,
he says.

It's hot in the sun,
and I roll up the sleeves
on my T-shirt.

He walks toward me
and his smile disappears.

What's that?
he points.

I don't know
where he's pointing—
at the wrinkled shirt
I slept in
or my hospital bracelet.

There,
he comes closer

and touches the inside part
of my right arm
between my shoulder
and my elbow,
you have bruises
on your arm,
blue oval bruises—
one two three
right there.

And a bigger one here,
his finger rests very lightly
on the spot.
There's a bigger bruise.
on the outside of your arm.
Do they hurt?
Did that happen
in the hospital?

I turn my arm
back and forth,
back and forth.
Alexander is right.
There are three reddish-blue spots
on one side,
and one bigger dark-blue oval
on the other.

I tap on them
with a finger,
and feel the tender soreness
under my skin.

And I remember—
down on the floor
twisting out of Mom's grip,
her fingers clenching
my arm.

No, not at the hospital,
I answer,
at home, before—
trying to pull away
from Mom.
She didn't like
that I was on the floor
picking up my papers.
It isn't anyone's fault.

Really?
Alexander says,
Not anyone's fault?
Like—I scraped my leg
getting it out of a shark's jaw.
Or—I tore my clothes
on the lion's claws,
Or . . .

I get it,
I interrupt,
I get what you're saying.
But my skin bruises easy.
It always has.
And I'm so pale,

it shows.
Really.

Really?
Alexander makes a face
that says
he's not buying it.
He acts more upset
than I am.

Really,
I say again,
a little less sure
this time.

Where was your father
when it happened?

Dad was outside.
He really loves my mom.
They're like those birds
that stay together
until one dies.

He makes another face.

That's an excuse?
That your parents are penguins?

Then Alexander lifts my arm,
and asks me what Isabel

asks Douglas
when he gets hurt,
¿Puedo hacerlo mejor?

I don't know
what the words mean,
but I know
what he's asking.

I nod yes,
and he bends his head
and gently kisses
each bruise.
One
Two
Three
Four

When he raises his head
our lips touch.
His press very softly
against mine,
as if he's afraid
to leave a mark.

MOM

Every few days,
Dad shows up at June's house
with tools—
rake, shovel, saw,
hammer, paintbrush, loppers.

He rakes up the wormy fruit
rotting under the apple tree,
trims the lilacs,
and replaces a broken windowpane
with new glass.

It's so sweet,
June says
when his car pulls in,
our Habitat for Humanity volunteer
is back again.

Today, instead of Dad,
Mom's car pulls up
to the Tibbettses' house.
It's the first time I've seen her
since I left home.

When she gets out,
I take a step back,
then stop.

I cross my arms
in front of me,
hiding the ovals
that are now a
greenish yellow.

I can't decide
what I feel—
if it's fear
or anger
or hope
or all of the above.

Is Dad okay?
I ask.

Your father is fine.
But it turns out those people in Arizona
made calls to the state.
Your sister, Ella, is in foster care
here in Maine,
and her caseworker
wants to set up a meeting.

One of Dad's ladders leans
against the roof of June's house,
where he started pulling
leaves out of the gutters.
I think how I'll never forget
where I was
and what I saw

when I heard
these words.

A meeting with me and Ella?
I say my sister's name
as if it cancels out
Mom saying it.

Yes, Mom says,
and Ella's foster mother,
and me and Dad, too.

No one asked me
if I wanted Mom and Dad there
when I met my sister
for the first time.

Where will we meet?

Ella's caseworker suggested
meeting at the foster mother's house
in Chester,
where she's been living.

There's a buzzing
in my ears.
Chester is where Mom works.
Dad goes there to buy the jars
for the garlic vinegar.
It's only two towns over
from Beacon.

It's like someone played a joke on me,
that my sister and I were so close
to each other all this time
and didn't know it.

And I thought you might be ready
to come home now.
So, why don't you grab your things
and we'll get going.

I say a silent apology to June
for the lie I have to tell.

I'd like to come home,
but June's having a hard time
and really wants me to stay
for a while.

Hmm, Mom says,
sorry to hear that
but I can't say
I'm completely surprised.
Those sisters of hers
are certainly not
the best role models.

When she gets back in the car,
Mom leans out the window,

Please thank Mrs. Tibbetts from us
for having you over.
And remember,

you don't want to overstay
your welcome.
We'll let you know
when the meeting is.

After Mom is gone
I keep thinking
about the way
she kept saying
Ella, Ella, Ella.

Each time she said *Ella*
she smiled to herself,
like eBay had given her
a second-chance offer
on an item she'd been watching—
a newer model that might be
more user friendly.

Even though the ground
is solid here,
and I can't taste any ash
in the air,
I'm scared.

I'm scared
that Mom wants to take
the one thing that's mine—
mia Sorella
mia Sorella minore—
and make it hers.

Sorella

My Sister Is Not a Baby

When Roshni tells me
I have a sister
she just found out about,
I'm all excited.

I always wanted
a baby sister
I could carry around
and push in a stroller
and teach how to talk.

This sister
is not a baby,
Roshni says.

She's seven years older
than me.
Her name is Rynn
and she got adopted
when she was a baby.
My mom
was also her mom.

I tell Roshni
I never heard
of someone named

Rynn.
I wouldn't name
a guinea pig
Rynn.
I don't even know
if I'll like her,
or if she'll like me.

Roshni takes a breath,
and it looks like
she's counting to ten.

*Do you want
to meet her?*
she asks.

*Does Rynn want to
meet ME?*
I ask Roshni.

She puts her hand
on my shoulder.
*Yes, she VERY much
wants to meet you.*

Okay, I say,
*I can show her
my lifebook
and introduce her
to Poker Face.
I hope she likes cats.*

When Mimi gets home
I'm gonna tell her
about my sister,
and say if this sister
likes me,
maybe one day
we can both go
to Camp To Belong.

PART
Three

Rynn

THE ONE HUGE WORD

Terence drives us all to Chester—
June next to Terence,
me squished between
her and Alexander
on the bench seat
of Terence's pickup.

Ella lives a block
from Giselle's Ice Cream Place,
and they'll wait for me there.

We're right on time,
but Mom's car
is already parked
in the driveway.
There's a trampoline
and a tire swing
in the front yard.

I knock,
and the door is opened
by a little girl
with a head
of black curly hair
holding a calico cat
in her arms.

The girl stares at me
and bursts into tears.
She drops the cat,
covers her face
with her hands,
and wails,

It's not fair, Martha.
How come SHE gets
to look like Mom?

A big woman with round glasses
comes and stands next to Ella.
She's wearing shorts and a blue T-shirt
that says "Camp To Belong Volunteer."

She kisses the top
of Ella's head,
but doesn't tell her
to stop crying.

Welcome, Rynn,
the woman says,
I'm Martha,
Ella's foster mom,
and this is your sister, Ella.

I can hardly breathe.
Sister feels like
the biggest word
in the universe.

Mom and Dad sit next to each other
on the couch.
Dad lifts a hand and waves hi.
Mom turns toward me,
but her eyes track Ella.

Finally, Ella stops crying,
sniffles a little,
and rubs her eyes.
She stares at me again.

Rynn is a weird name,
she says.

I kneel down near her
and pet the cat.

*Actually, my birthname
was Scheherazade
like your mom's.*

I say *your mom,*
because it doesn't feel right
to say *our mom.*
Ella had six whole years
with her,
and I had a few hours
or a few days,
or maybe not even that.

You got her name, too?
Ella's mouth opens,

and she looks like she's going
to cry again.

Not really,
I quickly say,
my parents changed it
to Rynn,
after my father's mother,
Rivka,
who died before I was born.

Ella glances over
where Mom and Dad sit,
and looks back at me,
like she has no interest
in who they are.

I never heard the name Rifka, either,
Ella mispronounces
my grandmother's name.
People called Mom Sherry,
Ella says.
Do you want me to call you that?

Sure, I'd like that,
I say,
imagining Terence's face
when he hears I have another
new name.

I think about telling her
Sorella means *sister,*

but I don't know
if that might make her cry, too.

I hold up the garlic bag
Dad brought me in the hospital.

I brought something for you.

Terence was the one who said
I should get Ella a present.

Sisters love presents,
he said,
I should know.
You better not show up
empty-handed.

I found a stuffed animal dog
at Goodwill.
It's a Saint Bernard
with a miniature barrel
on its neck.

Ella takes the dog
out of the bag
and strokes its fur.

How did you know
I like dogs?
she asks me.

I didn't know,

I say,
and the way it comes out
sounds so sad
and so true.

Ella swings the garlic bag
by its handles

I love this, too.
It's perfect to hold dog treats.
Do you want to take Martha's dog
for a walk with me?
We can bring along his treats in it.

Okay,
I say.

Come on, then.
Sherry and I
are taking Gravy
for a walk,
Ella announces
to everyone,
putting a leash
on a brown dog
that's asleep on the rug.

She sets the Saint Bernard
on a table,
and fills the garlic bag
with treats from a can

on the kitchen counter.

All the faces in the room
watch us
as I follow Ella outside,
as if they're thinking
the one huge word—
sisters.

WHAT ARE YOU GOOD AT?

The houses in Ella's neighborhood
are close together
and it's noisy—
kids playing in front yards
and backyards,
and more cars driving by
than I saw in a whole day
on Garlic Farm.
Ella waves to neighbors
and they wave back.

I'm taking Gravy and my sister
for a walk,
she tells them.

First, I thought
you'd be a LITTLE sister
I could help take care of,
Ella informs me.

That would have been fun,
I say.
I babysit a boy
who's almost two.

What's the boy's name?

Douglas.

Ella seems to think
that over.

Can I meet Douglas one day?
I could help you babysit him.

He would like that,
I answer,
and I picture Douglas and Ella
playing together in Water World.

Do you have a pet?
Ella asks me.

No, my dad is allergic
to cats and dogs.

What about fish?
Mimi has a betta fish.
Or mice, or turtles,
or a guinea pig?
Is he allergic to all of those?

I don't know,
I answer.

Hold Gravy's leash
for a minute.
Hold it really tight
and don't let go.
My dog, Storm, was hit by a car

and killed
when he got loose one time.

Ella hands me the leash,
and runs onto a lawn
with overgrown grass
and piles of branches.
She picks up different sticks
until she finds one she likes.
Gravy uses the time she's gone
to lie down on the sidewalk.

Here, Gravy.
She puts the stick on the ground
in front of the dog.
He sniffs at it,
chews on one end,
then picks it up
between his teeth.

What are you good at?
Ella asks me,
taking back the leash.

I have to think a minute.

I'm good at weeding, I guess.

Ella makes a face.

That's not a hobby.

What else?

Sewing. I can sew.

Can you sew ME something?

Sure. Like what?

Make it a surprise,
she says.

What are YOU good at?
I ask her.

Martha says I'm good at
making friends,
because I have a big heart.

When Ella says that,
I feel tears brim
in my eyes.
This little sister of mine,
all dark curls and bounce,
questions and confidence,
is happy in a way
I never was.
It's beautiful and it hurts,
and they both mix together
to make something
I have no words for.

Ella takes my hand
like she's the big sister.

Sherry, do you want me
to help you figure out
what kind of pet to get?

Yes, I squeeze her hand,
I would love that.

When we get back,
Ella drops to the ground
and crawls along
the side of the house,
then stops under the front window.

C'mon,
she whispers to me,
we can spy on them.

Gravy,
she throws the dog two treats
from the garlic bag.
You lie down
and be quiet.

We crouch together
under the big bay window.
Kids on bikes ride by,
and a mailman pushes a wheeled cart
down the sidewalk.

Ella leans against me.
Our shoulders touch,
and it makes me
catch my breath.

The weight of my sister's body
against mine,
the only person I've ever met
who's related to me,
though *related* doesn't feel
like the right word—
maybe *connected*
is a better word,
because it sounds more like
we're joined together
in a way no one
can take apart.

They're talking now,
Ella says,
and I wonder how often
she spies under this window.

Permanency plan . . .
Kinship placement . . . preference . . .
a true interest.
Ella and . . . strong bond.

Ella jabs my arm
with her elbow
when she hears her own name,

I knew it.
They're talking about me.
What are they saying?
she asks,
like they're speaking a language
she can't understand.

I don't know,
lots of big words,
I joke.

You're not a very good spy,
Ella says.

I guess not,
I admit,
should we go in now?

All right, Sherry,
Ella agrees,
as if she's letting me
have a turn
to decide
what we'll do next.

ELLA

Is that your father?
Ella points to Dad,
who's still sitting on the couch
in the living room
next to Mom.

Yes.

My dad's in Windham State Prison,
Ella says.
For a long, long time.
He was in a fight,
but it might not be
his fault.

Oh, I say.

Ella goes over
and stands in front
of Dad,
her hands on her hips.

Hi, are you allergic
to mice?

No, not that I know of,
Dad answers.

What about fish?

Allergic to eating fish?
Dad looks confused.

No, like pet fish
in a tank of water,
Ella explains.

No, I'm not allergic to fish.

What about turtles
or guinea pigs?
Are you allergic to them?

No, I don't think I am,
Dad says.

He sounds like he hopes
he's giving Ella
the right answers.

SEE, I TOLD YOU, SHERRY.
YOU CAN HAVE A PET!
Ella pumps her fists
in the air.

Ella, honey,
Martha says,
she needs to discuss this
with her parents first.

Martha holds her arms out
to Ella,
who goes over and sits
in her lap.
Ella seems kind of big
to be sitting in laps,
but she puts her arms
around Martha's neck
and whispers in her ear,
loud enough for everyone to hear,

I was just trying
to be NICE.
She doesn't have ANY pets
at all.
I wish Sherry lived HERE.
Then she could have
whatever pet she wanted.

After she speaks
all the grown-ups are quiet
and no one looks at each other.
Martha's face is hidden
behind Ella's hair.
Mom and Dad each look
at opposite walls in the room.

It's as if no one wants to say—
that's not how the world works, Ella.
You don't get to decide
who has a pet,

where your sister lives,
or even what will happen
to you.

A-hum,
Mom clears her throat.
Hi, Ella,
Mom says,
I'm Leanne Parkman,
and this is my husband, Saul,
Rynn's parents.
I actually work right here
in Chester.

Well, I LIVE in Chester,
Ella answers.

Would you like to take
a walk with me?
Mom asks Ella.

I already went for a walk—
with Sherry,
Ella says.

When Ella says that,
I don't think anyone but me
notices how Mom
presses her lips together
so they almost disappear.

Her red lipstick is smudged
and she looks uncomfortable
in Martha's house,
like she's sitting in detention.
I sort of feel sorry for her
and for once, I don't care
what she does to me,
but I worry about Ella.

I start talking loud
to get Mom's attention
away from Ella,
but I act like I'm talking to everyone
in the room.

I saw a big yard sale
down the street.
There's a lot of dishes
on the table.
Some of them looked old,
I add,
because Mom collects antique
teacups.
I think you can see it from the window.

I even point in the direction
of the window,
but Mom doesn't get up.
She crosses one leg over the other,
and taps her foot
in the air.

Dad smiles at Ella.
You remind me of Rynn
when she was your age,
he says.

Why? She has straight brown hair
and I have black curly hair.

Dad smiles even bigger
at that.

It looks like you have a gold tooth,
Ella peers into
Dad's mouth.
Is it real gold?

Yes, it is gold.

WOW, Ella says,
you're lucky!

When I first noticed them,
I also liked the gleams of gold
in Dad's teeth,
and his stories about the dentist
who used a foot-powered drill.

It's hard to concentrate
when Mom and Dad are talking
to Ella,
so I look around the room.

There are shelves filled with photos
of kids,
and my heart skips a beat
when I see my birthmother's face
in a red-and-purple frame.
It's like a time-travel picture of me
ten years from now.
There's also a big picture of a man
over the couch.

When we get ready to go,
Ella starts crying again.

I never got to show Sherry
my lifebook,
she sobs to Martha.

Oh, sweetheart,
Martha says,
think how much fun it will be
to show her at your next visit.
Maybe you can add some things
to it before then.

Okay,
Ella stops crying
and wipes her nose
on the back of her hand,
but don't forget, Sherry,
about what you're gonna bring ME
next time.

She makes needle-and-thread
sewing motions with her hand.

I won't forget,
I say.

And think about what pet
you want,
she adds.

I will,
I promise.

When Mom and Dad and I
are outside,
Mom turns to Dad,
I think that went well.
And Martha seemed to imply that Ella's father
was ready to relinquish his parental rights.
We'll have to discuss that
with Ella's caseworker.

I like Martha.
She seems really nice,
I say.

Mom lowers her voice,

You do know, Rynn,
that Martha gets paid
to take care of Ella.

I do, I answer,
but I don't say
what is so obvious
no one could miss it—
that the bond between Martha and Ella
has nothing to do
with money.

THE VERY FIRST PHOTO

Everyone is there waiting
in Giselle's Ice Cream Place.

Did she like the present?
Terence asks first.

She adored it.
Thanks for the tip,
I say.

How was it?
What happened?
June makes her big-eye face.

Well?
Alexander says softly,
hanging his arm
over my shoulder.

I lean against him.
There are no words
to say what it was like,
so I hold up my phone
and show them the photo—
the very first photo
of me and my sister—
both of us huddled under the window,
our two heads touching.

She's beautiful,
June gushes,
look at those eyes.

I can see who's gonna be
the boss sister,
Terence jokes.

You're both making
the same face,
Alexander observes.

I look again, and it's true.
We both have an expression
that says—
we're hiding out together,
no one knows,
how fun is that?

Now that I've met her,
I can't imagine a sister
any different
than Ella.

That's what it must feel like
when a mother sees her baby
for the first time—
surprised and not surprised
by who she is.

Now I have two things

on my to-do list—
teach Douglas
how to play
hide-and-seek
and sew something
for Ella.

HIDE-AND-SEEK

Wanna play a fun game
with me and Alexander?
I ask Douglas.

Yop,
he says,
his version
of *yep.*

It's called hide-and-seek.
You have to cover your eyes
and count to ten.

I demonstrate
with my hands
over my eyes.

Don't think
Douglas can count
all the way to ten,
Alexander points out.

New plan, Douglas,
I say,
I'm gonna close my eyes
and count to two.
One two, one two,
one two, one two,

and you and Alexander
are gonna hide.

Alexander slow-motion runs
and hides behind a big oak tree
on the lawn.

Count wit Win,
Douglas stands by me
and covers his eyes, too.

New plan, Alexander,
I say,
Douglas and I will count
and you'll hide.

Hide in tree,
Douglas observes.

Yes, but we'll close our eyes,
and Alexander will hide
somewhere else
this time.

It feels like I'm
putting on a play
and no one,
including me,
knows their parts.

Douglas covers his eyes
but keeps them open

and peeks out between
his fingers.

One two, one two,
one two, one two,
one two,
I count.

READY OR NOT
HERE I COME,
I yell.
Can you say that, Douglas?
ONE TWO,
he yells,
ONE TWO,
and runs right over
to Alexander,
hiding behind a sheet
on the clothesline.

One two hide,
Douglas calls out,
and runs behind
the oak tree.
FIND ME, WIN.

Not bad for a
first game.
I think he gets
the general idea,
I tell Alexander.
Do you think Ella

is too old
for hide-and-seek?

Everything I do now
makes me think
about Ella.
Would she want
to hide
or seek?
Would she cry
when she was found,
mad that someone figured out
her hiding place?

Never too old
for the game,
he says.
Aren't we playing it?

Find ME, Scheherazade.
He covers his eyes
with splayed-out fingers
like Douglas,
please find me.

And I cover my eyes
with spread-out fingers, too—
my gray eyes very close
to his brown eyes
so there's no place
for either of us
to hide.

PROBLEMS

Do you want to hear
my problem?
I ask June one night.
We're both lying
in our beds.
The room is dark
except for the fairy lights.
I don't wait
for her to answer.

Ella wants me to have a pet,
but I don't want anything
in a cage,
or a fish that can only
swim in circles
in a bowl,
I tell her.

You're missing the whole point
of a pet,
June says.
A pet is not a wild animal.

I don't care.
I don't want anything
that's trapped.
A mouse running back and forth
against glass walls?
No.

Turtles stuck
on a little plastic island?
No.

Okay, I get it,
she says,
you want a pet
'cause Ella wants you
to have a pet,
but you want that pet
to be free.

Yes,
I say,
I guess I want a pet
that's not a pet.
I want something alive
but I don't want to
boss it.
I want it to be
equal to me.

Then that would be
a human pet.
Wait a minute—
I think I have a brother
who would be just right
for the job.

I throw May's pillow
at her.

Then she pulls something
out from under her mattress
and throws it at me.

That's my problem,
she says.

I unfold the square of paper
and read what it says.
Then I sit up in bed.

Wow, June!
You got a scholarship
to the science and math high school!
Congratulations!
What did your mom say?

No one else knows.
She sits up, too.
It's so far away—
five hours north to Limestone.
And we'd still have to pay
toward room and board.
It's probably too late to go,
anyway.

I reread the letter
that congratulates June
on getting in,
then try to smooth out
the folded creases

of the paper.

You should go
if you want to go,
even though I'd really miss you.
But you'd get to take classes
they don't have here in Beacon—
all that advanced science and math.

I know, and I'd get to see who I am
when it's just me,
without my whole family around.

Then June looks up at the ceiling.
Remember when I didn't tell Alexander
what my two words were?
That's 'cause I was thinking
they were scared *and* selfish.
It would be selfish of me
to leave Mom and Terence
and the rest of the family,
and I'm kinda scared to go.
Doesn't everyone hate
the one who leaves?
It's like you're saying
it isn't good enough
where you are.
Besides, now you're here,
sister July.

June suddenly realizes
what she said.

Ooh, stupid me.
I didn't mean you leaving home.
Everyone loves you.
And you had to leave.

I guess June did know
more than I thought—
the way true friends do.
And I love how she says
You had to leave
in such a matter-of-fact way.

It's okay.
I knew what you meant,
I say.
I'd miss you if you left,
but I could help your mom out
and keep Terence company.
Though my mother said I shouldn't
overstay my welcome,
I say.

The word *overstay*
and its opposite,
stayover,
have been going
round and round
in my head
ever since Mom said it.

June tosses the pillow
back at me.

Did she?
Would you like to know
what two words
I think about that?

SKY-BLUE CURTAINS

Over the past two weeks,
Dad brought
my toothbrush,
my hairbrush,
and some of my clothes.
When I ask for something,
he gets the garlic account book
from the van
and writes it down
on a back page:

Gray hoodie
Computer
Sneakers

Today he holds his pen
in the air when I ask
for my sky-blue curtains.

Your curtains?
From your room?
Are you sure?

Dad started painting the shutters
on the front of the Tibbetts farmhouse
and Terence is helping him today.
Terence keeps working
while I talk to Dad.

The back windows are south facing,
so it will be hot for you
in the summer without curtains,
and they also stop drafts
in the winter months,
Dad explains.

I think about how to answer.
I don't want anyone
to feel bad
because of me—
even Mom,
and especially Dad—
but cave women
have to be all about survival.

I can't come home,
I say.

And I'm sixteen,
I add, which is a random fact—
just like Dad's tutorial
about the seasonal benefits of curtains—
that has nothing to do
with what we're really talking about.

Besides, I promised to sew something
for Ella.
And I thought I'd use
the curtain fabric,
since it's so pretty.

All right,
Dad takes a breath so deep
it makes him cough.

Then he starts making a list.
I'll bring thread and scissors
and pins.
I'd planned to give you
my mother's electric sewing machine,
as a going-away-to-college present,
but you can have it now.

Terence has his back to us,
paintbrush in his hand,
and I hear him choking
on his laugh
about Dad's plan
for my college gift.

Dad still has the typewriter
his parents gave him
when he went to college.
It weighs about a hundred pounds
and comes in its own suitcase,
so it could have been
much worse.

WRONG ANSWER

Sewing looks like a
one-person job,
Alexander watches me
thread the sewing machine,
which sits on a card table
Mrs. Tibbetts set up
in the living room.
Is there anything I can do
to help?
Anything, of course,
except run my fingers
under the needle.

You can pin these two fabrics together,
I hand him pieces
of cut-out sky-blue fabric
and a tin of pins.

Today Dad is painting the shutters
on the back of the house.
He waves at me and Alexander
on his way up
and down
the ladder.

I can't believe
he keeps finding
more and more things
to do here,

I say,
as Dad's legs
make their way up
again.

Why do you think that is?
Alexander asks,
stabbing pins through the cloth
like they're darts.
I take back the pieces
and show him the wavelike
in-and-out motion
that keeps the pins
in the fabric.

*He's paying Mrs. Tibbetts back
for all the breakfast cereal I eat?*

Alexander makes a
wrong-answer buzzer sound.

*Guess again, Scheherazade.
You know her better than I do.
Has June's mom ever cared
that the paint on her shutters
was flaking off
or her rose arbor was tilting
slightly to the left?
You don't think she knows
it's his way of still being
part of your life?*

Oh, I say,
and I realize June and Terence
also probably figured this out
before me.

The other day
I broke it to him
that I'm not going back home,
I say.

Alexander looks up from the fabric,
a pin in his hand.

How did he take it?
Do you think he knows why?

I remember the deep breath
Dad took when I told him.

He was kind of inscrutable,
but I think he knows,
I say.

NOT THE POTTY TRAINING STORY

In July
it feels like summer
will last forever.
The farmers market
is full of new potatoes,
early tomatoes, and string beans.

I try not to think
about Alexander
and maybe June—
leaving.
Or the big words I heard
under the window
at Martha's house,
and what Mom said
about Ella's father.

One evening, back from work,
Mrs. Tibbetts watches me sew
on Dad's mother's machine.
It's black with gold decals
on the edges,
and makes a quiet *ber ber ber* sound
when the wheel turns.

My next meeting with my sister
is in two days,

and I'm busy making
her presents.

How's it going, Rynn?
Mrs. Tibbetts asks.

Good, I say,
*there's so much fabric
I keep coming up with
more things to make.*

I show her the present for Ella
and the one for Gravy.

Those are really nice.
You're very talented.
But I meant,
how are things going
in general?
I know it gets crazy here, sometimes,
with the family in and out
and April coming around
with her kids.
I can't seem to get ahead
of the mess.
You must miss the quiet
at your house
and your dad's cooking.
He was telling me about
a dish he made the other day—
it had spices
I never heard of.

My hands freeze
at the sewing machine.
I lift my foot
off the pedal.
The words she says
change shape in my mind.

You don't want me
to stay?
It's too much work?
Too much food?
Francine from the farmers market—
the one who sells cheese—
might let me live with her.
I could ask.

Rynn, how could you think that?
Mrs. Tibbetts looks horrified.
You've been part of this family
since you were a baby.
I remember when I had my daycare,
you and June and Terence
played so sweetly with each other.
You even potty trained together.

WAIT, MOM,
June rushes into the living room
with a stop-sign hand
in the air,
DON'T START THE POTTY TRAINING STORY
WITHOUT ME AND TERENCE.
OH, TERENCE,

YOU DON'T WANT TO MISS THIS!
June's teasing voice
draws Terence downstairs,
and he stands in the doorway.

Sorry, Rynn,
June says,
I know you've heard it before,
but it's especially embarrassing
for Terence.
Right, Terence?
Mom's telling the Wee Ones
potty training story.
She's almost to the part
where you were a whole year older
than me and Rynn,
but we trained first.

Oh yes, that story.
Terence goes over to Mrs. Tibbetts.
This won't hurt, Mom,
he teases her,
I'll hold your hand,
and June will erase your memory.
It will only take a minute.

Mrs. Tibbetts giggles like a little kid
and reaches up to pull Terence's face
down for a kiss.

I can't help laughing, too,

and an answer
to one of Mrs. Tibbetts's questions
comes out,

I do miss garlic,
I say.
Dad cooked a lot
with garlic.

Mrs. Tibbetts beams
at me,
Of course you do, Rynn.
You practically grew up
on garlic.
The fact is,
I never ate garlic
a day in my life.
Onions and chives
but never garlic.
I wouldn't know what
to do with it.
Your father must have eaten it
when he lived in New York City.

This happens to Dad
all the time.
Whatever he does,
whatever he talks about,
it's like he's wearing a hat
that says "New York City" on it,
and that's all people see.

Maybe that's how Uncle Curt feels
about his photo on Cops & Courts.

Spaghetti with garlic and oil
is really easy.
I could make it for supper sometime,
I offer.

Mrs. Tibbetts goes into the kitchen
and comes back
with one of Dad's garlic bags
full of garlic.

Your father brought me this
last week.
It's been sitting in the back
of the fridge.
Do you mind if I keep the bag, though?
It's awfully cute.

Sorella

No

I listen from the stairs
when Martha talks
on the phone.

It's just as well.
A prison is no place
for a little girl.
And I don't believe in
the goodbye visit anyway.

Sherry is coming tomorrow.
The man with the gold teeth
is coming, too,
and the lady who's always
mad.

Yesterday Mimi surprised me
with word stickers
to decorate my lifebook.
They say things like
AMAZING and WOW.
I stuck an AMAZING one
next to the photo of me
right after I was born,
and a GOOD TIMES one
under the picture of me and Mom
at the beach.

After we look at my
lifebook,
I'm gonna ask Sherry
if I can style her hair.
And then we can go
to Giselle's Ice Cream Place.

Martha says that's a lot
for one visit,
and did I remember
how we talked about
taking NO for an answer.

NO,
I say,
I don't remember that
at all.

LIFEBOOK

For visit number two with Ella,
Terence drops me off
on the way
to a firewood delivery.

I get there at one
instead of two
on purpose
so Mom and Dad
aren't here yet.

Ella is waiting
on the sidewalk
in front of the house.
Gravy lies in the shade
under the one tree
on the front lawn.
Ella has a hairbrush
in one hand
and a comb
in the other.
She shakes them
in the air.

Can I style your hair?
After I show you

my lifebook.
I washed my brush
and comb.
Martha says you can sit
in her swivel chair,
so it will be like
you're in a real salon.

I don't know
what it is
about my hair
that has Ella
so excited—
if it's because it's long
and straight,
instead of short and curly
like hers
or that it's
the same color
as our mother's hair.

Sure,
I say,
that would be fun.

I'm not gonna cut it,
she says,
just style it.

Good to know,
I say.

When we go inside,
Martha is in the kitchen.
She doesn't say
I'm an hour early.
She serves iced tea
and apple juice.
I pour from the iced tea
pitcher.

Juice is better.
Why do you like
iced tea?
Ella asks me.

I don't know.
I just like the taste.

Ella watches me drink
from my glass,
then pours herself
an inch of iced tea,
and makes a *yech* face.

She leads me
into the living room
and points to a binder
on the coffee table.

That's my lifebook,
she says,
Mimi helped me

decorate it yesterday.

She opens the lifebook
to the first page.

Under an AMAZING sticker
a woman with long brown hair
cradles a baby
in her arms.
She's looking right into
the baby's face.

That's me,
Ella says,
see my hair.
I was born
with so much hair
Mom could put it
in a barrette.

That's me.
See, that's me,
Ella turns page
after page,
pointing to the
black-haired baby
who gets bigger
and bigger.

The woman with brown hair,
dark-gray eyes, and pale skin

is alive in the lifebook.
She and Ella are at the beach.
She and Ella are at the zoo.
She's holding Ella up
to blow out birthday candles.
Other stickers say
WAY COOL
SHINE BRIGHT
BEST DAY EVER.

In my mind,
I ask my birthmother,
I see you,
do you see me?
Where were you
all that time,
all my birthdays?

Some pages have a man
with a beard
carrying Ella,
and some pages show
a large yellow dog
I'm guessing is Storm.

I can't
look away,
but every time
Ella turns a page,
I feel more and more
invisible—

like my life
is a fake life,
and the one
in Ella's pages
is real.

Ella sits very close to me,
and when I take a drink
of iced tea,
she takes a little
sip of hers, too.
I really wish
the multiverse theory
June told me about
was true—
that there's a parallel universe
where my birthmother
is my mother
AND Ella's mother.
That somewhere
there's a lifebook
with my face in it, too.

Ella gets to the last page
and closes the book.
She turns to me,
puffs out a big sigh
and says,

I guess you forgot, huh?

Forgot what?

Forgot you were going to
sew me something.

My backpack is on the floor
next to the couch.
I pick it up and unzip it.

I didn't forget.
I have them in here.

MARTHA, I TOLD YOU
SHERRY WOULDN'T FORGET
TO SEW ME SOMETHING,
Ella yells to Martha,
even though she's just in
the next room.

I lay the gifts on Ella's lap
one at a time—
all of them made with
curtain fabric.

First, a headband for Ella,
then a matching bandanna
for Gravy,
and last,
a little cloth mouse
(stuffed with dried catnip
from the farmers market)
for Poker Face.
I explain who gets each one
and what they are.

When Mom and Dad arrive,
Ella is wearing her headband,
Gravy's bandanna
is tied around his neck,
and Poker Face is sniffing
the sky-blue mouse.

Ella spins me back and forth
in the swivel chair,
while she spritzes my hair
with a spray bottle of water.
It feels like a crazy warm rain
falling on my dizzy head.

Don't come in the room.
I'm doing her hair.
You can't look yet,
Ella calls out
to Mom and Dad and Martha.
She starts brushing my hair—
long, slow, gentle strokes
from the very top
all the way down.

You know what,
she says to me,
I'm starting to like iced tea, too,
just like you.

ALL THE WORDS

As far as I can tell
without a mirror,
my new style consists of
a lot of bobby pins
stuck in my hair.

Ta-da,
Ella announces
the big reveal,
twirling me around.
I expect bobby pins
to shoot out
in all directions,
but they stay in place.

Very lovely, Ella,
Martha smiles.
*Should I take a picture
of the two of you?*

Yes!
Ella poses next to me
with the brush
in her hand,
and Martha takes photos
with her camera.

Mom and Dad stand there

like they came late to a party
they didn't know
was happening.

*Why don't you show
the Parkmans your lifebook,*
Martha suggests to Ella.

*I already showed it
to Sherry,*
Ella says,
*and my fingers are tired
from turning the pages.*
She bends the fingers
of her right hand
into a stiff claw.

It feels like a secret sister thing
is going on—
that Ella is reading my mind—
and can tell
what I want
what I don't want,
without me saying
a word.

I have a better idea,
Ella says,
*why don't we all walk over
to Giselle's Ice Cream Place?*

300

Ella is first
down the road,
telling Mom and Dad
her number one
(peppermint stick)
and number two
(cookies and cream)
ice cream choices.

I hang back
next to Martha.
I remember the first visit
when she held her arms out
and took Ella in her lap.
And how Ella was
happy and sad and mad
all in the same hour,
and Martha's expression hardly changed.
It was like,
instead of judging her
for every little thing she did or said,
or every face she made,
she just saw inside Ella
to her good heart.

It makes me wonder
what I'd be like
if Mom had seen me that way.
If I'd be the kind of person
with the confidence
to speak her mind

and show what she really feels,
without always thinking about
the consequences.
If I'd be as strong as June
as funny as Terence
and as honest as Alexander.

Everything
I've been wanting to say
waiting to say
afraid to say,
comes out.

I know what my mom's trying
to do.
Don't let it happen.
It would not
be good.
Please.
Don't let her
take Ella.

Martha stops right there
on the sidewalk.
I've gone this far,
and I can't think
of any other way
to protect Ella.
There's no time to wait
for a spell
or a curse
to be broken.

So I give Martha
all the words.

Look at her,
how HERSELF she is,
I point ahead of us
to Ella skipping along
in her sky-blue headband.
Mom would take all that
away.
No matter what Ella did,
or how hard she tried,
it would never
be good enough,
I say.
Tell everyone—
if they talk about
"kinship placement."
I air-quote two of the big words
I heard under the window,
I don't even live
with Mom and Dad
anymore.

Martha's soft hand
touches mine,
and she says something
no one ever said to me before,

You're a very good sister.

Sorella

Martha

I forgot to ask Sherry
if she decided on a pet.
If she picks a box turtle
I'll dig it worms
in the backyard.

I'm making
a surprise gift
for my sister.
It's a lot of work,
so I hope she
appreciates it.

Martha's white sneakers
are walking a little faster
on the treadmill.

*When are you going
to run?*
I ask her.

*That would be
never,*
she says.

Martha has a chart

to remind her to eat
fruits and vegetables.
She's supposed to have
five a day.

We still have pizza-night Fridays,
but now Martha adds broccoli
to her slices.

I wondered if a really big apple
would count as two fruits
or if that would be cheating.
Martha said she could ask
her doctor about that.

I spied Martha
talking to her husband Blaine's picture
in the living room yesterday.

Please give me a sign,
I heard her say.

Today I told Martha
not to worry
about Blaine—
that my mom
was looking after him
in heaven.

PART

Four

PART
Four

COCOON

Dad found a rope hammock
in Mrs. Tibbetts's shed
and strung it between two pine trees
at the edge of her back lawn.

Ever since Ella showed me her lifebook,
I see captions for everything I do.

Today's is:

Me + Alexander
in a hammock

We both fit in the hammock,
hip to hip,
leg against leg.

The bruises on my arm
have bright-yellow halos now,
like someone circled them
with a highlighter.
They don't hurt to touch anymore,
but I notice Alexander is still careful
not to bump into them.

The branches above us

are full of pinecones.
Dad says trees put out more cones
when they're stressed.
So many things
can stress a tree—
too little rain or too much rain,
really cold nights
or hot days.
I close my eyes
and breathe in the smell
of pine.

So, there's a law
about getting emancipated
from your parents,
Alexander says.
When you're sixteen
you can apply to the court,
and they'll give you a free lawyer.
If the court says yes, your parents
won't be the boss of you at all.
Legally, they wouldn't even be
your parents.

I understand what he's saying
and why he's saying it,
but I think about Dad waving at me
going up and down the ladder
outside Mrs. Tibbetts's window.

Yeah, but can you imagine

my father's face
if I tried to explain that to him?
Or could you picture him
in a courthouse,
hearing from a judge
that I wasn't legally
his daughter anymore?

I see what you mean,
Alexander says.

We're both quiet then,
rocking the hammock
back and forth.

How's work going
with Terence and his dad?
I ask.

It's hard but it's good.
And what's weird—
all these years
even though the doctors said
good-as-new
about my fingers,
I thought if I ever really
worked hard with them,
they might fly off
like fake fingers
that were only glued on.
But they don't.

When Alexander says
fake fingers,
it reminds me how I felt
looking through the pages
in Ella's lifebook.

I reach out with both hands
and pull the sides
of the woven hammock together
so they meet in the middle
above us.
This tilts us
toward each other.

Alexander and Scheherazade
both completely real
in a hammock cocoon,
I say.

Alexander with Scheherazade
in Beacon, Maine,
only one more week,
he says.

I let the hammock sides go.
You're leaving?

I half hoped
or full hoped
he would stay,
since pretty soon

he'd be sixteen
and could decide for himself.

There's my mom,
and school,
he says.

I never met his mom,
but it could be like me
not wanting to tell Dad
I'm *emancipated.*

I never really liked being here
before this summer,
he says,
lacing our hands together.
It made me think
if the accident hadn't happened,
this would still be my world—
on the farm with my parents,
instead of in an apartment
in the city with my mom.
And when Douglas was born,
it felt like he would get to have the life
I should have had.

Then I saw how hard you tried
to find Ella,
and how good it was
when you did.
I'm gonna use the money from

working with Terence and his dad
to come back here on my winter break.
I don't want Douglas—or you—
to forget me.

It's too bad
there's not one place
where everybody you love
could always be—
some tiny planet like the one
the Little Prince lived on.
Then you'd never have to miss
anyone.

I lean over and kiss
his warm, nonbionic lips.
I won't forget you,
I say.

UNCLE CURT

Douglas wants to play
hide-and-seek
all the time,
but he only wants
to hide.

He has two hiding places—
one is behind the oak tree,
the other is under the picnic table.

He squirms around
in his hiding spot,
so excited for us
to find him.

And every time he's found,
Douglas yells BOO,
like he was the one
to find US.

I've given up
trying to explain
the rules
for hiding.

I'm not hiding, either,
the way I was before.
I may not be *emancipated*,

but it doesn't mean
I can't act like it.

It started when Alexander said,
It helps to call things
by their right names.

After that, I met my sister
and got to see her fearless
say-what-she-thinks personality
in action.

Then I stood there
on the sidewalk
and told Martha
the truth.
Now I can't stop.

When I FaceTime Uncle Curt
I forget that nine a.m. in Beacon, Maine,
is seven a.m. in Phoenix, Arizona.
Uncle Curt is in a kitchen
that looks like it belongs
in a cooking show.
And behind him is the biggest living room
I've ever seen—
a whole wall full of windows,
and white fans spinning
from the top of a very high ceiling.

Scheherazade,
you're calling early.

What's up?
he asks me.

My parents are taking
foster-to-adopt classes
to get licensed to take Ella.

I quickly explain
what I learned online.

When you're a relative,
even if you live in another state,
you can apply for kinship care.
You might get priority,
since you're her uncle.
They'd have to do a home study,
but it looks like you have a great home.
And if you come to Maine to meet her,
you'll love Ella.
Plus, she's really good with dogs.

Can you hold on a second?
Uncle Curt asks,
and sets the phone down.
For a while, all I see is a row of
shiny copper hanging lights.

Just had to get some coffee,
he says when he gets back on.
He has a mug in one hand.
It looks like the coffee is black.

I'm not understanding, Scheherazade.
How is it a problem
if your parents adopt Sorella?
I thought that's what you wanted,
why you tried to find her—
for the two of you to be together.
And I thought the meetings
with your sister
were going really well.

I'm out of hiding,
so I say what he and Aunt Kissy
never thought to ask
about my life,

Things are bad with my mom.
I'm not living at home anymore.

Uncle Curt laughs this weird laugh
that sounds more like
he's coughing.

I'm sure you'll work it out.
What teenager gets along
with their mother, right?
Kissy has her hands full
with the boys,
and summer is when a turf doctor
makes his money.

Then he cough-laughs again,
and adds,

as if it's the punch line
of a joke,

*Gotta keep 'em green
to make the green.*

That might be funny
to a sod specialist,
but not to me.
I gave him my words
and he gave me a joke.

I don't wait
for his answer.
I don't kiss the tips
of my fingers
and wave them at him.

Instead, I say,
It's your loss,
press the red *X*
on my phone
to disconnect,
and then neither of us
is there.

MAINE'S WAITING CHILDREN

My command-central attic research
into "foster care" and "Maine"
turns up the "Sibling Bill of Rights."
It was signed in Maine in 2012.
There are six *whereas*es in it.
This is number five:

"Whereas: sibling separation is a significant and
distinct loss
that must be repaired by frequent and regular
contact;"

Below all the *whereas*es
there's a list
of ten things
every foster child
shall have.

Number four is:

"Shall be actively involved in his/her siblings' lives
and share celebrations including birthdays, holidays,
graduations, and meaningful milestones."

I also find the website
"Meet Maine's Waiting Children."
It has photos of kids in Maine
who need a family.

I scroll down,
afraid I'll see Ella
on their list.

There are twenty-three kids
on the website.
The youngest one is eight,
and the oldest is seventeen.
Sixteen have smiles
that show teeth,
four have turned-up mouth smiles
with no teeth,
and three have straight-line smiles.
I'm not sure why this bothers me
so much—
that someone told them to smile
for the camera,
to give them a better chance
for a family.

There are so many names:
Coralynn, Jerold and Joseph,
Doria, Ilana, Michael, Troy.
Some have a brother or sister
and want to stay together.

I read the descriptions
of the children:

"Coralynn loves sports
and has a lot of energy."
"Doria likes riding her bike

and playing Legos."
"Ilana is a motivated student."
"Joseph loves horses
and would like to maintain contact
with his half brother and father."

I try to imagine
what they'd say about Ella:

"Ella loves animals.
Ella likes peppermint-stick ice cream.
Ella is good at spying.
Ella would like to maintain contact
with her sister, Sherry."

How could these sentences
or even a photo
explain what it feels like
when Ella puts her sweaty little hand
in mine?

GLITTER WORDS

It must be more secret sister
mind-reading—
Dad says Ella wants only me
for visit number three
this Sunday.

Will I ever stop counting
the times we meet?
Or when we're both old,
will I greet Ella and say
how this is our two thousand
five hundred and sixth visit?

Dad drives me there
and Martha comes out to say
she can take me back.
Neither she nor Dad
say where *back* is now.

Ella points to the blue headband
she's wearing,
and at Gravy,
following behind
in his bandanna.
She jumps up and down.

I made YOU something
this time, Sherry.

Bet you can't guess
what it is.

I have no idea,
I agree.

There's a man watching us
from Martha's front window.
When we go inside,
he introduces himself.

I'm Willis, Ella's GAL.
He says each letter
one at a time,
Gee-Ay-El.

Ella's *gal*,
whatever that means,
doesn't look much older
than Terence,
and he's wearing a blue-and-white
Hawaiian shirt.
The skin across one cheek
and part of his chin
is thick and ridged.

It's okay to look
at his face,
Ella informs me.
He got hurt in a fire
when he was little.
Right, Willis?

That is true, Ella,
he says.

And he got adopted
when he was twelve.
I can tell that
'cause it's not a secret,
Ella adds.

What's a gal?
I ask him.

Gee-Ay-El stands for
guardian ad litem.
A gee-ay-el is the eyes and ears
of the court,
serving the best interests
of the child.

Willis (six letters, TWO repeats,
and two real words)
taps his eyes
and then his ears
as if I didn't know the difference
between them.

HERE,
Ella hands me a package
wrapped in red tissue paper,
and covered with about a hundred stickers
that say:

HOORAY
WOW
ADORABLE
FABULOUS
OUTTA SIGHT
AMAZING
HIGH FIVE

WOW, AMAZING,
I say, using two of the sticker words.

Thanks, I used the whole rest
of the sticker book
Mimi gave me.
She said it was up to me
what I did with them.

Should I open it now?
I ask.

Yes, she says,
touching one of the
YES stickers on the package,
open it on the couch.

Ella probably used
a whole roll of tape
to wrap my present.
While I unpeel it,
I feel Willis's
eyes and ears on us
across the room,

like he's turned on
the video camera
in his eyes,
and the voice recorder
in his ears,
implanted there
by *the court*.

It's a notebook
with words that sparkle
in red and gold glitter
on the cover.

Big letters that say:

Sherry's Lifebook

Look inside now,
Ella directs me,
so impatient
she rocks back and forth
on her toes.

On the first page is the photo
Martha took of the two of us
at our last visit.

Around the photo,
drawings of a dog with a stick
in his mouth,
and a cat playing with a
blue mouse.

Underneath it,
in more sparkly letters—

Ella + Sherry

The instant I see those words,
I know I will never forget
this moment,
and I wish my birthmother
was here to see them, too.

I trace our names
with my finger.

It's perfect.
I really really love it.
You did a great job,
I say,
and turn to give her a hug.
She hugs me back,
her arms tight around my neck.
Willis's eye camera
records it all.

After Ella showed me
her lifebook,
I read about them online
on the foster care website.
Sometimes a lifebook starts
at the time a child's old life
is gone, and a new one
is just beginning.

I used glitter pens,
she says,
and you can add more things
if you want.
Why don't you take a picture
of us now?

When I get my phone
from my pack,
there are five missed messages
from Alexander.

Five texts that say:

"douglas is lost."

"he was right there
in the yard
with Isabel."

"then gone."

"your dad and police
on the way. Terence
and his family
are here."

"please come
help find"

FAULT

Martha shakes her car keys,
Let's go. I can drive.

I'll help navigate,
Ella's gal says,
*I know a shortcut
to Beacon.*

Ella and I sit together
in the back seat.

Does Douglas have a mom?
Ella asks me.

Yes, he does.

Then she'll find him,
Ella pats my knee,
*and will we pass your house
on the way?
Tell me if we do
so I can see where you live.*

Willis glances back at us,
all *eyes* and *ears*,
when Ella says that.

Umm,
I say.

Do you like Douglas
more than me?
Ella asks.

I know how a grown-up
would answer her question—
explaining how everyone is special
and we can appreciate
all the wonderful things
about each person.

But Ella is looking at me
with an expression I recognize.
She's ready to hear
that she's second best.

Of course not.
I like Douglas, but
I like YOU even more.

Ella tries to hide
her satisfied smile.

I've got my fingers and toes crossed
for Douglas,
she holds up her crossed fingers,
then takes her sandals off
and lifts her feet

to show me her crossed toes.
I look ahead out the window
without really seeing anything
because I know this is
all my fault,
just like it was me
searching for my birthmother
that put Ella
in Mom's way.

When Isabel hired me
to watch Douglas,
she said,
Just keep him safe.

I taught him
hide-and-seek
and I'm the one
who said to Douglas
last week,

Hey, big guy,
isn't it time to find a new
hiding place?

And the other thing I said.

You have to be real quiet
when you hide, Douglas,
so no one can find you.

I hope Ella understands
I can't get a pet.
I can't have one more thing
to keep safe.

SEEK

Everyone at the farm
says the same things
over and over.

Where could a little boy
hide?

Anywhere.

How far could he have gone?

There's farm as far
as you can see.

What was he wearing?

Only a diaper.

An almost two-year-old boy
could be in a shed
full of tools,
behind leafy tomato plants
in a greenhouse,
or in the bucket
of a tractor.

¿DOUGLAS, DONDE ESTAS?
Isabel cries out.

DOUGLAS,
Martha, who never met him,
calls his name.

WHERE ARE YOU, DOUGLAS?
Willis, the eyes and ears
of the court,
yells, running behind the house.

DOUGLAS, MY BOY,
I HAVE CANDY FOR YOU,
June shouts from the front porch,
the last place Isabel saw him.
Douglas's plastic pool, water toys,
slide, and balls are all still there
on the lawn,
as if they're waiting for him
to return.

Mrs. Tibbetts triple-checks
all the rooms and closets
in the house.

Isabel wraps her arms
around me, and weeps hot tears
onto my neck,

I said, Douglas, can you play
hide-and-seek by yourself a minute
while I help these people
at the farm stand?

What was I thinking?

We'll find him,
I hug her back,
and she tells me
Big Doug and Alexander
are out searching
in rows of corn,
tall enough to hide
a little boy.

In the crowd of seekers,
I watch my sister's people
meet my Beacon people,
something I never imagined
would ever happen.
It's like the connect-the-dot game,
where you keep connecting dots
until they make a whole picture.

Terence dot connects to Ella dot,
June dot connects to Martha dot,
and Willis dot connects to
Mrs. Tibbetts dot.

Who's that?
I hear Willis ask Mrs. Tibbetts,
pointing to Dad,
who's standing completely still
in the middle of the crowd,
his head tilted

to one side,
like he's listening
for a signal
that will give him
the coordinates of a child
on a farm in Beacon, Maine.

That's Rynn's dad,
she says.

WORST-CASE SCENARIOS

It's muggy and hot,
and deerflies bite
the back of my neck.
I forgot sunscreen today
and my face feels as red
as the tomatoes
in the farm stand.
Mrs. Tibbetts brings out
glasses of water
from the house.

Two of Beacon's volunteer firefighters
show up right before the police.
April and May come
with April's children,
and Ella runs over
to the kids.

Hi, I'm Ella. I'm nine.
I came with my sister, Sherry.
Let's all help look for Douglas.
Maybe he climbed a tree.

I see what Martha meant
about my sister's big heart
being good at making friends.

Suddenly, Mom is there too,

talking to the volunteer firefighters.
She must have been in my
blind spot,
because I didn't see her arrive.

Her voice is loud enough
to carry across the yard.

Doesn't a stream run through
the back of this land?

Couldn't a coyote drag off
a small child?

I'm glad Isabel
went inside the house
with the police officer,
and is not here
listening to Mom's
worst-case scenarios—
Mom thinking up the ways
a child could be lost or taken
seems *deliberately cruel,*
like she's sure
Isabel's boy will end up
as a black-and-white photo
in the bottom
of a jewelry box.

Everyone around Mom
stops talking,

as if they can't believe
what they're hearing.

A freaking coyote?
Who is THAT?
Willis asks me,
making a face
that doesn't seem
very professional
for a gee-ay-el.

I look right at him
so he can see my
extra-high eyebrow raise.

That would be
my mom,
I answer.

Now Dad is crawling
on the lawn
around the house.
There was a poster
in the hospital elevator
about the warning signs of a stroke.
One sign was trouble walking.

Dad is crawling with his elbows stuck out,
his body close to the ground
like a tadpole that's grown short arms
but no legs.

Mom hasn't moved an inch
to look for Douglas,
but as the firefighters back away
from her, she adds,

What about empty refrigerators?
Or rain barrels?
And isn't there a junk truck
out in the woods?

As I search behind the farm stand,
and recheck Douglas's favorite
hiding spots,
and look under cars—
instead of bad things,
I imagine all the good things
that could happen
to him.

I picture Douglas
coming through corn stalks
on Big Doug's shoulders,
and I think of the new games—
inside games
like making blanket forts
under a table,
and building block towers—
I'll teach Douglas
when he is found.

FOUND

I stop for a minute
and look up at the sky—
the one quiet place
no one searches.
Turkey vultures circle above,
like they're hunting too.

I'm sorry, Douglas,
I'm so sorry,
I speak to him
in my mind.

Suddenly, I hear screams
from the other side of the house,
and I think of Mom's
worst-case scenarios
coming true.
I run toward the screams
in time to see Dad pulling Douglas out
from the incredibly small space
under the porch.

Douglas's diaper
hangs almost to his knees,
his face and belly
smeared with dirt.

The door to the house
bangs open,

and Isabel sobs
as she runs to take him
from Dad.
Douglas, mi hijo,
she lifts him into her arms.
Why didn't you answer
when we called?
Don't EVER
do that again.

June holds her phone up
to take a photo
of Douglas and Isabel.

What the hell, Douglas,
June says,
do we need to put a tracking chip in you?

Got candy?
Douglas puts his hand out.

Isabel turns to Dad,

Saul, how did you think
to check under there?

Dad looks down
at his sneakers.

I thought about
where Rynn
used to hide.

I drop onto my knees,
and my tears
make the world blurry.
It's too much
all at once.

Douglas is safe
and Dad knew
all along
that I hid
from Mom
under the porch.
He saved Douglas,
but he never saved me.

And right there on the ground
I decide I'm going to save
anyone I can.
It won't matter if I've known them
a day or a year or their whole life—
I'll never choose one person
over the other,
no matter who they are.

Dad is suddenly surrounded by people
shaking his hand
and congratulating him
and then he's gone with Isabel and Douglas
into the house.

I'm still on my knees
when I hear Mrs. Tibbetts speak,

Leanne, she's your daughter,
go to her.

You're damn right
she's my daughter,
Mom snaps,
but she doesn't come over
to me.

Instead,
she steps closer
to Mrs. Tibbetts.

But you don't seem to realize that, do you?
Haven't you got enough
druggie daughters to keep track of
without trying to make me look
like a bad mother?

No one is judging you, Leanne,
Mrs. Tibbetts says.
We all do our best.

Mom steps forward
and shoves her in the chest.

And you have my husband
coming over and fixing up
your house.
What's that all about?

Terence gets between them.

He holds his hands up,
and looks directly at Mom,

Do NOT touch my mother again.
No one is trying to make you look bad.
His voice is quiet but firm.

That's right,
you're doing it all by yourself, Leanne,
May says.

I hear April's squeaky voice.
Remind me to take Mrs. Parkman off my list
of character references for drug court,
she draws out the syllables in *Mrs.* and *Parkman.*

Girls, please,
Mrs. Tibbetts scolds them gently,
tipping her head in my direction.

Behind them I see June
still holding up her phone,
and Willis in his Hawaiian shirt
standing with Martha
watching it all.

Mom turns away
and heads toward her car.
When she passes Water World,
she kicks Douglas's plastic ladder
out of her way.
It falls on its side

and she gives it one more kick
to clear her path.

Then she gets in the car
and tears out of the gravel driveway
in swirls of dust.

Ella runs across the lawn
to where I'm still on the ground,
and squats in front of me.

Get up, Sherry.
Didn't you see?
Douglas is found!
Don't be sad anymore.

Martha is there, too,
wiping my eyes with her fingers.
They both help me up.

Okay, Ella,
I say,
and as if her words are magic,
I feel my sadness disappear.

June and Terence and all the Tibbettses
gather around us.
It's over, June says to me,
and I don't know if she means
Douglas's disappearance
or Mom's scene.

Terence pats my head
like I'm a puppy,
as the police loudspeakers
shout Douglas's return,
and Alexander and Big Doug
come running out of the cornfield
and into the farmhouse.

All the fear
on the farm
turns to joy—
Douglas, Douglas, Douglas,
people cheer.
Willis claps and joins in the chant.
It's the best-case scenario
anyone could hope for.

Isabel comes to the front door
and calls out,
Listen up, everyone,
we happen to have
two strawberry rhubarb pies
sitting on the counter.
You're all invited in
to share a slice,
and celebrate the safe return
of our little runaway
and a happy ending
to the longest hour
of my life.

Did you hear that, Sherry?
There's pies,
Ella tells me.

In the house,
Isabel hooks her arm
in Dad's,
Our biggest thanks
and the biggest slice
to our friend and neighbor—
Saul Parkman.
Isabel hands Dad a plate of pie.
You're our hero,
she says,
nuestro héroe.

Everyone looks at Dad—
the police officers, volunteer firefighters,
Martha, Ella and Willis,
Mrs. Tibbetts and her daughters
and grandchildren.

Dad surprises me
by answering Isabel in Spanish—
making her nod and laugh—
but even with my one year of Spanish,
I can't understand a thing.

If this was a fairy tale,
Isabel and Big Doug
would be rulers of a kingdom,

and Douglas their little prince.
They'd give Dad
a wish-come-true
for saving their son.
He'd choose to break
Mom's spell,
and it would all be
happily-ever-after.
But it's only Beacon, Maine,
so Dad gets the first piece
of pie.

That was some smart thinking
on your part,
Willis says to Dad,
I'm impressed.

Dad puts his fork down
on his plate,
Thank you very much.
I can say I've found,
when searching,
that you have to think
of the probable,
not just the possible.

June catches my eye,
and I know what's she thinking—
Dad is definitely being *inscrutable.*

Did they teach you search and rescue
back there in New York City?

one of the firefighters jokes.

We will never forget this.
Big Doug is holding Douglas,
and his voice breaks
when he speaks.
We will never forget
how you came together
to look for our boy.
And now if you'll excuse me,
I'm going to get him
cleaned up.

I take a plate of pie
and find a seat at the farmhouse table.
The pie is so good I eat it slowly
to make it last—
the sweetness of the strawberries
covering the sour taste of rhubarb.
I watch Ella laughing with the kids,
and helping to pass out plates of pie.

I hear June talking to her mother
on the other side of the room.

I got into the magnet high school
up in Limestone,
and if I can, I want to go.

Mrs. Tibbetts wraps June
in a big hug.

We'll make it work,
she says.

Good for you, June,
you deserve it,
May says,
and she and April
turn it into a Tibbetts group hug.

I see the happy and sad
in Terence's face.

He comes over
and sits with me.

You're not planning on leaving, too,
are you, sister July?
he says,
taking my fork
and scooping himself
a piece of my pie.

No, not me,
I answer.

Then Alexander is there,
hugging me,
Thank you, thank you,
he says in my ear,
like it's me who found Douglas.
What a crazy last day here.

352

That's right,
you're leaving tomorrow.

Yeah, Dad is taking me to the airport
early in the morning.

Alexander looks so much happier
than the first time I met him,
getting out of Isabel's car
with his suitcase,
and I want to say something more
than just goodbye.

But before I can speak,
Douglas runs into the room,
his hair wet and his face
all scrubbed and shiny.
He sees me and screeches, *WIN.*
I bend down and pick him up,
and hold him as lightly
and as tightly
as I dare.

Sorella

A Hundred Million Times

I made two new friends
at Douglas's farm,
a boy and a girl,
and Douglas's big brother
showed me the chickens
and the pigs.

One of the chickens
liked being cuddled
and didn't want me
to put her down.

Yesterday, Willis came over
with Dunkin' Donuts,
and Martha had half
of a glazed blueberry doughnut,
even though it's not a real fruit
and doesn't count
for her five a day.

Willis said Dad is sorry
he'll be in jail even longer
because of the fight.
I knew what Martha was thinking
so I said it before she did.

That's why we use our words, right?

Then I said that Sherry's mom
started a fight
at the farm,
but *she's* not in jail.
And she didn't even help Sherry
get up from the ground.
Me and Martha had to do it.

Willis and Martha
looked at each other.

*Do you want to stay here
with Martha?*
Willis asked me.
Roshni says you do.

I told him
that's what I've been saying
about a hundred million times,
but no one listens to me.

Then Willis stared at me
without even blinking,
and said,

*I'm listening, Ella,
I'm listening.*

Rynn

SPY

I'm in the kitchen
when I see June and Terence
sitting on the porch,
looking at her phone.

Hashtag bad behavior,
June says.

Hashtag don't blame the slide,
Terence says.

Hashtag kick it once, kick it twice,
says June.

Hashtag kiddie pool is next,
says Terence.

They both look guilty
when I come outside.

Show me,
I say,
sticking my hand out.

June gives me the phone.

There's the video she took
of Mom kicking Douglas's slide,
then kicking it
out of her way again.

I watch it
over and over
but it's never funny
to me.

Sorry, I'll delete it.
I didn't send it to anyone,
June apologizes.

Someone else was there at the farm
taking pictures,
probably a reporter,
because the next day
Douglas's photo is on the front page
of the paper
along with the story
of his lost and found.
He's covered in dirt
and wearing his droopy diaper.

There's a smaller photo of Mom
shoving Mrs. Tibbetts
with the caption:
"Beacon woman assaults neighbor
after missing toddler found."

Alexander flew back home
the day after Douglas was found,
and soon June is really going away
to the science and math school.

Guess what?
June says.
Your father
paid my room and board.
He said it was only fair
since you're staying here.
Mom tried to refuse,
saying he couldn't make that much money
selling garlic and garlic vinegar,
but your father told her he had a pension
from his work in the OICI.

June pauses for effect.
OICI,
if you didn't know,
stands for Office of Intelligence
and Counterintelligence.

It turns out Terence was right—
Dad *was* a spy.

MESSAGES

Message One:

Hi, Uncle Curt,
this is Scheherazade.
I wanted to say I understand
if you can't adopt Ella.
I know Arizona is far
from Maine.
I actually looked it up
and it's almost three thousand miles.
You probably know that already.
Well, I hope you get
this message.
Call if you want.
I'm here.
Bye.

Message Two:

Hi, Uncle Curt,
It's me,
Scheherazade.
Don't know if you got
my last message.
Or if it got lost
in your work messages.
I hope Brayden and Kaden
are doing okay,

and Aunt Kissy, too.
If you've been away on vacation,
and just got back,
don't worry about calling
right away.
I'll be here.

Message Three:

Hi, Uncle Curt,
this is Scheherazade.
I'm doing good,
and so is Ella.
And my dad's garlic
is almost ready to harvest.
I don't even know
if you can grow garlic
in Phoenix, Arizona.
You'd probably have to water it.
Or irrigate it, right?
Dad says it's time to pull
when there's two dead leaves
on the plant.
Then we tie bunches together
with hay string and hang them
under the eaves to dry.
I don't know how I got talking
about garlic anyway.
I don't know
if you even like garlic.
Well, summer is almost over.

So give a call if you want.
Bye.

I never hear back from Uncle Curt,
and finally, I text Aunt Kissy.

"Is everything okay?
Uncle Curt isn't answering
my messages."

Kissy texts back right away,
and it's like she took the words
from a bad breakup scene.

"It's not you.
It's Curt.
He's having a hard time
with this whole reunion thing.
He tried to put the past
behind him.
So sorry.
Please stay in touch.
XOXOX"

Isn't the past already
behind him?
That's how the past works.
And what does *please stay in touch* mean—
leaving more messages
on a phone
that never picks up?

Below the "sorry"
there are four sad emojis.
Is it one for each of them—
Curt, Kissy, Brayden, and Kaden?

I look for an emoji
to text back.
None are exactly right,
but I choose the face
with two eyes
in its yellow circle
but no mouth or eyebrows
to give away
what it's really feeling.

SELF-SERVE

I haven't babysat Douglas
since he was lost and found
and Alexander went home.
I trust you, Isabel said
when I called,
but I'm too nervous
to let him out of my sight.
Please stop by.
He keeps asking for you.

When I go to the farm
things look different.
First of all,
Douglas isn't outside
to screech at me
when I show up,
the Water World pool
is empty,
and none of Douglas's toys
are on the lawn,
as if no child lives there
anymore.

Also, the farm stand sign is changed.
Now it says "Self-Serve"
so people who stop
are on their honor
to weigh the vegetables they want

and leave their money
in a quart canning jar
labeled "Pay Here."

When I knock on the door,
I hear the turning
of a latch,
and a chime goes off
when the door opens.

It's an alarm,
Isabel explains,
letting me in.

All of Douglas's outside toys—
even his slide—
are in the living room.

WIN,
Douglas shouts.
He's strapped in a high chair
that looks brand-new.

DOUGLAS,
I shout back,
and he laughs,
offering me cut-up food
from his tray—
slices of cheese, blueberries, squares of toast.

Isabel watches me eat

Douglas's shared food,
doing a silly slurp-lick
with each bite.

Thanks for coming, Rynn,
she says,
gracias.

It's the first time
Isabel said anything to me
in Spanish.
Even if it's only the one word,
it feels like she's showing me
what's in her heart.

I could say I understand
what it's like
to find someone you thought
was lost to you,
or to lose someone
you never got to know,
but I don't.

De nada,
I say,
and Isabel smiles in surprise.
I've decided to take Spanish II
this fall so I can learn more than
two words.
*I like what you've done
to the house.*

KEY

Dad brings a bag
to Mrs. Tibbetts's house
with the things from home
on my latest list:

Purple sweater
School binders
Calculator

And then,
he gives me
one more thing,
so small it fits
in the palm of my hand.
It's metal with grooves
on one side.

Here's a house key for you,
in case,
Dad explains,
standing next to the van.
Mom is taking a leave of absence
from work,
and we're planning a trip.
A change of scene
could be a good thing for her.
We might be gone awhile,
so I left paperwork with Mrs. Tibbetts

if you need permissions for school
or to see the doctor.
And of course we'll have our phones
with us, so you can call anytime.

I close my fingers
over the key.
We never locked
the door,
so I didn't know
there even was a key
to the house.

I put it in my pocket
and stand there wondering
if "in case" is
Dad spy code
for something else?

In case
I need more thread and pins?
In case
they don't come back?

It shouldn't come as a surprise
that Dad is choosing
what's best for Mom,
even if it means
leaving me,
but it still doesn't seem fair.
Maybe the Home for Little Pilgrims
forgot to ask my parents

the most important question
of all—
If there was a choice,
who would you save?

I don't know
what Dad tells himself.
That she needs him
more than I do?
That he's always done
what he thought was best
for the whole family?

Or is it some kind of old-fashioned loyalty
I'll never understand,
something he learned
growing up in the Bronx—
from his own father,
or even the grandfather,
who delivered glass bottles
filled with seltzer
from a wooden truck?
Did they say children
are like scrappy dogs,
able to look out for themselves,
and who'll eventually leave home,
so put your bet on your wife?

Even I know
not everything parents tell you
turns out to be true.

I thought you were both taking
those foster-to-adopt classes?
I ask.

We stopped the classes—
with what happened
on the farm.
And the piece in the paper . . .

He doesn't finish the sentence,
and I remember Willis
with his *gee-ay-el* eyes and ears.
I don't know what it takes
to be a gal,
but that's a job I might like—
where what matters
is to *see* and *hear*
what no one else
wants to recognize,
and do something
about it.

Then Dad reaches into
his front shirt pocket.

I almost forgot.
This is a debit card.
If you want . . .
He stops and seems to be thinking
about what I might want.
New winter boots, or socks,
or that Twizzler candy you like so much.

Thanks, Dad, I appreciate it.

He covers my hand
that's now holding the key
and the debit card
with his own hand.

You have a good time with Ella.
You're both lucky to have each other.
And don't worry about your mother.

Does he mean don't worry,
Mom can't hurt you anymore,
or don't worry, I'll take care of Mom—
or both?

When we hug,
I feel the bones
in his arms and spine
through his shirt.
The skin on his face is soft
and smells like garlic.

I know he's old,
but this is the first time
I think about a world
with him gone from it.

Am I going to see you again
before you go?
I ask.

We'll stop by before we leave,
Dad says,
but you've got the key,
as if now that he's presented me
with the *key,*
I'm a junior spy.

PACKING

June's packing
is a family project.
Her suitcase and bags
are spread out on the floor
in the living room,
and all the Tibbettses and Trues
come by with going-away presents.

May gives her a beanbag chair.
Her father brings over
a mini fridge he got
at a yard sale.
Grammie Tibbetts shows up
with a jumbo jar of malted milk balls.

People, I'm sharing one half
of a dorm room,
not moving into a condo,
June says
when Grammie True
hauls in her standing craft light.
My roommate is gonna have
a hoarder intervention
my first week of school.

You need good light,
Grammie True insists.

I give June two gifts.
One is a sky-blue pillowcase
sewn from my curtains.
I stitched crisscrossed *X*s
all along the edge
so June will always be
exactly where she wants.

There was enough fabric
to make a pillowcase twin
for May's bed, too.

I used my babysitting money
for the other gift—
the longest string
of fairy lights
to light up her ceiling
at school.

Mrs. Tibbetts watches June
without saying a word,
like she's memorizing everything
about her.

June waves to her mom
from across the room.

You're leaving,
Mrs. Tibbetts sighs.

Yes, Mom, I'm leaving.

I'm only going to northern Maine,
not the moon—yet.
To a school in the middle
of potato fields.
And they send me home
every month
for a long weekend.

I know that, June,
Mrs. Tibbetts says,
her puppy-dog eyes
still tracking June's every move.

I have something
for you, too, Rynn,
Grammie True takes a
cardboard box out of her purse.
I read the words on the front.

"Welcome to your
23andMe
Ancestry
saliva collection kit."

On the back it says,
"Learn what your DNA
says about you."

My nephew gave it to me
for Christmas.
It was nice of him,

but I don't see myself
spitting in a tube.
You might be able to find
more folks out there
related to you,
she says.

Thank you,
I say,
happier Grammie True
thought of me
than about getting my very own
saliva collection kit.

Sorella

My New Name

When Mimi goes to Camp To Belong
with her brothers,
I go to day camp,
and Martha goes to Silver Sneakers
at the gym.

Silver Sneakers is the name
of Martha's new exercise class.
Your sneakers
don't have to be silver.
She uses weights.
I asked how heavy
and she said two pounds.

That's not very heavy,
I laughed,
a kitten weighs
two pounds,
and anyone can lift a kitten.

It's a start,
she said.

Martha's lawyer
is helping her
adopt me.

She has to fill out papers
and have a new
home study.

Once everything is done,
we'll go to the court.
It might take six months,
but Martha hopes
only three.

In the court,
the judge will ask questions,
like do you know
what adoption means.
I can talk too.

Then everyone signs
the adoption certificate
and it's done.
Martha asked do I want
her last name,
which is York.
I thought about it
and said yes,
'cause that's what it says
on our mailbox.

Martha said it was fine
to have both last names.
So when it's my turn
to talk,

I'll tell the judge
my new name is gonna be
Sorella Buzzell York.

Rynn

VANISHING POINT

Leaves are changing colors—
yellows and reds and oranges—
and the nights are cool.
I'm back at school,
the bus now picking me up
on Tibbetts Road.

Terence and I are outside
throwing firewood in his truck.
After Alexander left,
I got his job.
Now I work with Terence
on firewood deliveries.
His extra gloves are big on me,
but they keep out the splinters.

*I've been thinking
about your sod specialist uncle,*
Terence says,
*and I got the idea to start my own
lawn business—
something to do
when firewood is slow.
Maybe one day I could afford
an in-ground pool like his,
and a cement slab all around it.
What do you think?*

I think I want to be the first one
in the pool,
I say.

Even when I didn't notice,
Terence has been there—
driving me to the Maine Home
for Little Pilgrims
and to my first visit with Ella,
standing between Mom
and Mrs. Tibbetts,
staying
when June and Alexander left.

Terence stops tossing wood.

It looks like your parents
are here,
he says,
as an RV with tinted windows,
towing Mom's car behind it,
pulls up in front of June's house.
If you need my referee skills,
give me a wave.

He dances back and forth
with his hands out,
as if he's refereeing imaginary people.
His buzz cut is growing out
and it makes him look like a
baby duckling.

Will do,
I say.

I get to the RV
just as Mom and Dad climb down
from the cab.
Mom's hands are behind her back.

We're heading out
on a trip cross-country,
Dad says.
I can't be sure,
but I think he winks
at me.

You're gonna live in this?

I point to the RV
and the word VAGABOND
painted on the side
in black letters.

Yes, it sleeps four,
Dad says,
has a gas stove and a fridge,
a TV and a microwave.

We don't have a microwave
in our house,
but Mom and Dad
have one in the

VAGABOND.
It feels like a fairy tale
where someone was given
impossible tasks
to prove their love—
like finding a ring
thrown into the vast ocean.

Only here the tasks are—
say goodbye to the land
you've made your home,
drive a metal monster
of a house on wheels
across the country,
and leave your only child.

Dad never winked at me before,
so I hope the wink
I might have seen
means Dad has a plan
as *precise* and *inscrutable*
as June thinks he is—
a plan to drive Mom
across the country
to find the pure waterfall
or healing rock
that can break her curse.

I hear the thuds
of Terence throwing wood
in the truck,

and smell the chimney smoke
in the air,
and I understand what it means
when people say
Time stood still.

When will you be back?
I ask them.

I don't know,
Mom says.
*A cousin of mine
thinks my mother settled
out in California.
So we'll see about that.
And keep your grades up, Rynn,*
Mom adds,
I can still check them online.

I think of the perfect three-word answer—
You do that.

But there are dark rings under Mom's eyes,
like smudged charcoal,
and she bites into her own bottom lip
the way I do when I'm stumped
by a hard math problem.

I hope you find her,
I say,
and I mean it.

I know what it's like
to want your mother,
no matter what happened.

Here,
Mom sets the paper bag
she was holding behind her back
in front of me.

It's fabric,
she says.
*Someone at work was cleaning out
her craft room.
I told them my daughter
loves to sew.*

I open the bag
and look through the fabric.
There's a green piece,
Ella's favorite color,
that's perfect to make something
for her tenth birthday.

Thank you,
I say.

Then we all stand there
and no one seems to know
what to do next.

So I say what Dad said

before my eighth grade class
went on its end-of-year trip
to Washington, DC.

Have fun,
I say.
Send a postcard
if you have time.

Then I kiss the tips
of my fingers
and wave them
at Mom and Dad.

When the VAGABOND pulls out
from the curb,
I can't tell if Mom
is looking back at me,
but I stand very still
just in case.

The farther they go,
the smaller the motor home looks,
and I imagine myself shrinking, too,
until Mom can't see me anymore.

In art class,
they had us do the same thing—
draw a little figure
on top of our paper,
with road lines leading to it.

They called it
the vanishing point.

I used to watch for motor homes
parked in people's yards
or on the highway.
I liked that they were a home
you could take with you
anywhere you wanted.
I've seen ones called
CHALLENGER
HURRICANE
SOLITUDE
and INFERNO.
So VAGABOND
is not that bad.

NAMES

Ella is okay
with me not having
my own pet.
She gave me a glitter coupon
for a half share
in Poker Face.
She says when I visit,
I can pet Poker Face
as much as I want,
but I also have to clean
her litterbox.

I spit in the tube
Grammie True gave me.
Four weeks later,
I have five hundred and thirteen
DNA relatives
on 23andMe,
even if they mostly share
only tiny bits of chromosomes.

I also get proof of my cave-woman genes,
with a report that says:
"Hey, Rynn!
You have more Neanderthal DNA
than 72% of other customers."

Martha has a court date

for the adoption
a month from now,
and I'm invited to go.
Ella says when it's her turn
to talk,
she's gonna tell the judge
her new name.

If the judge asks me
my name,
I'll say each of them,
one after the other:

Rynn
Garlic-Girl
Scheherazade
Babysitter
Win
Grande Sorella
Sherry
July

Uncle Curt still hasn't called back.
On my birthday,
Aunt Kissy texted me
balloon, cake, and heart emojis,
and I texted back
a thumbs-up and two pink hearts.

When I'm eighteen
I'll go to the Maine Home

for Little Pilgrims,
and maybe my birthfather's name
will be somewhere
in my file.

There might also be a letter
from my birthmother
waiting for me,
saying why
she couldn't keep me.

She gave me her name
and she gave
my sister, Sorella,
a name with a clue.

So I believe
she wanted us
to find each other.

And for now,
that's good enough.

GARLIC

I go back
to Garlic Farm
for the first time
since I left,
my house key
tucked deep
in my pocket.

Some nights,
in May's bed
under the fairy lights,
I dream about going home,
but I can never
get there.
The road bursts into flames,
or the people I ask for directions
can't understand
what I'm saying.

The garlic garden
is covered with compost,
and there are wooden stakes
with the names of the bulbs
to mark the straight rows—
Glenora Pearl, Music, Orchard Hill
Siberian, Persian Star, Georgian Fire,
German Extra Hardy, and
Elephant.

This year I wasn't there
to help drop the garlic cloves
into the deep furrows
Dad made,
and cover them up
for winter.

I'm guessing this means
he plans to be back in time
for harvest.

Then I notice
a newly tilled patch of dirt
beyond the garlic
with plastic nursery tags
nailed to stakes
at the end of each row.
"Jersey Giant Asparagus"
"Purple Passion Asparagus"
"Millennium Asparagus"

Not only does Dad plan
to be back,
but he's starting
a new crop.

I take a photo of the spot
and text it to Alexander
with the words
"Soon to be Asparagus-Girl."

Then I touch the key
in my pocket
and look up behind me
at my bedroom window,
strange and bare
without any curtains.

I don't go inside,
but before I leave
I slip my feet
out of my flip-flops—
not to test for tremors
but just to feel the green grass
alive with crickets
between my toes.

PUMPKINS

Everyone with a name pumpkin
is invited to Francine's
Pick Your Pumpkin day.

I'm going with Martha and Ella,
and Isabel is coming with Douglas.
Douglas shows up
at the pumpkin patch
with black canvas straps
clipped around his waist
and over his shoulders.
Attached to them is a longer strap,
and Isabel grips the end of it
in her fist.

Ella runs over to them.
Hi there, Douglas, remember me?
I'll help you find your pumpkin.

Can I hold his leash?
she asks Isabel.
I promise I won't let go.

Isabel gives the strap to Ella,
but follows close behind them.

Douglas starts with D.
We have to look
for a D,

Ella explains to Douglas.

The sky is the clear blue
you get in the fall.
This is our twelfth visit
with each other,
and today's caption is:

Ella + Sherry
in the Pumpkin Patch

For our eleventh visit,
Martha asked me
what I'd like to do.
I thought of what it said
about Scheherazade "Sherry" Walker
on Legacy.com,
"She loved camping
and the ocean,"
and made my choice:

Ella + Sherry
at the ocean

It was windy and cold
at the ocean,
but we got our feet wet,
picked rocks and shells,
and yelled back at the waves.
Martha says next summer
we can go camping.

It's windy and cool
in the pumpkin patch, too.
We had a hard frost
the other day,
and the pumpkin leaves
are shriveled up and black,
but all the pumpkins
are bright orange.

In the middle of the patch
there's a really big pumpkin
marked "Zoe"
still on its vine.
If Francine's daughter
finally comes home,
I hope it's in time
to see her name pumpkin.

I find my pumpkins first.
RYNN and SCHEHERAZADE
are growing on the same twisty vine.
They're both the size of basketballs
and have long curvy stems.
I touch the words
that are my names.
You could call the raised letters
lines or prints or scars or defects,
but to me it's always been magic—
that my name could grow
on a pumpkin.

Isabel finds Douglas's pumpkin
and is so happy,
it's like she's found
Douglas himself.

*I think the KIDS are supposed to find
the pumpkins, NOT the grown-ups,*
Ella tells Isabel,
one hand on her hip.

*And can you please
take Douglas's leash now?
I want to find my pumpkin,
and my arm hurts
from him pulling.*

I see Francine suggest a corner
of the patch for Ella to look in,
and soon after, Ella's excited cries
carry across the field.

*See, everybody,
I found mine,*
Ella shouts,
and then she tells everyone
what I explained to her
in the car
on the way here.

*My pumpkin says Ella,
not Sorella.*

That's because
Sherry didn't know
my real name
was Sorella.

And you know what
Sorella *means?*
It means sister
in Italian.
If you don't believe me,
you can look it up,
'cause it's a fact.
Right, Sherry?

The two words
I think of
when I watch Ella
hug her name pumpkin
with both arms
are *sister* and *safe.*
Two words
that are also
my words now.

Yes,
I say.
It's definitely
a fact.

Author's Note

I was nine months old when I entered foster care, and I lived in several different foster homes before being adopted three years later.

Mine was a closed adoption through the now-defunct Louise Wise Agency. Their methods, in many aspects, have since come under scrutiny. I was told my birth parents were cancer researchers, too busy with their work to raise a child. Growing up, I imagined them in a laboratory, wearing white coats and bent over a microscope, always *this* close to a cure for cancer.

You might think I was a pretty gullible child to believe that story, and you would be right. But it seemed as plausible as anything I read in the books I loved—Sara Crewe's only remaining parent dying of *brain fever* on another continent or Meg Murry's father disappearing into a wrinkle in time.

As an adult, I was able to obtain "nonidentifying" information from my adoption records. I read about my time in foster care and the true occupations of my birth parents.

Then, when a state adoption registry opened to biological siblings, I matched with a sister I didn't know I had. Suddenly I had five younger siblings—three sisters and two brothers—who'd known about my existence their whole lives. They helped my birth father search for me for years, even contacting the adoption agency, but were falsely told the records had been destroyed in a fire. There were many surprising discoveries and coincidences. One sister and I had gone to the same college. Another sister had the same name as my daughter. And we grew up in towns as close as eight miles apart but never crossed paths.

Meeting my siblings was amazing and emotional. It was also bittersweet, as we were all grown up and had missed sharing a childhood together. When I met their father, my birth father, I brought with me the only baby photos of myself that I'd been given from before my adoption. It turned out they were part of a set taken by a photographer when I was three months old. My birth father had kept the other half of the photos and we put them together for the first time since I was a baby. And during our conversations, I found out more details about my entrance into foster care and subsequent adoption.

Later on, through a DNA test, I connected online with other biological relatives across the country. One person directed me to a 1938 film, taken by a great-uncle, that's archived in the United States Holocaust Memorial Museum. It shows my maternal birth great-grandparents in Poland before their deaths in 1942.

Over the years, every new fact, even those that were hard to hear, gave me back another missing piece of my history. And they made me think even more about what it means to be adopted, what family is, as well as how we try to protect ourselves and the people we love. And while Rynn's story is not my story, my personal experiences inspired the book.

Thank you so much for reading!

Sincerely,
Betty Culley

Acknowledgments

To my brilliant editor, Tara Weikum. I'm overjoyed to work on a second novel with you. Thank you for holding this book of my heart in your skilled hands and helping me to shape it into its final form.

With appreciation to associate editor Sarah Homer, copyeditors Alexandra Rakaczki and Megan Gendell, designers Julia Feingold and Alison Donalty, artist Kimberly Glyder, and to the whole team at HarperCollins.

To my agent, Steven Chudney, whose offer of representation was the beginning of more than I ever imagined. I'm so happy to be on Team Chudney.

Nora Sosnoff, child protective division chief, Office of the Maine Attorney General, for her legal expertise.

Shannon Flood, friend and longtime foster parent in Maine, for her support and information.

Gale Davison, career child protective worker in Maine, for helpful feedback on the manuscript.

Jeffrey S. Dolley, Esq., for insight into the work of guardians ad litem and foster parenting.

Adoptive parent, foster parent, and kinship placement provider Rockie Decker and adoptive and foster parent Anna Anderson for sharing their experiences.

Camp To Belong for the good work they do in their mission to reunite siblings who have become separated in foster care through a week of camp in the summer and other events throughout the year.

Thank you to critique group writers Cathy McKelway, Sally Stanton, and Melanie Ellsworth for your friendship and inspiration.

Heartfelt thanks to Susan Davis Moore, Eileen and Bill Culley, and Eric Boulton-Bailey for their support, and to early readers Vickie Limberger, AnnMarie Limberger, Greta Limberger, Sylvane Pontin, Ray Pontin, Wesley McNair, Yolanda Kolinski, Ann Dorney, and David Axelman.

To my aunt, Gerry Teitelbaum, who calls me by my original name, for her kindness.

With love and gratitude to my sister Barbara for finding me, and to my brothers and sisters, Michele, David, Gerry, and Rachel, for welcoming me into the family.

For my daughter, Rachel, for her steadfast belief in this novel.

And to Denis for being that true home.